Praise for Brenda L.

Fourpl

"If y'all thought *Threesome* wuz hot, *Fourplay* iz off da chain!"

—Shannon Holmes, author of *B-More Careful* and *Bad Girlz*

"Provocative, sexy, daring . . . Sasha is a wild and interesting character."

—Buck Tharp, contributor, *People* magazine

"Sasha is back. . . . She's a strong, beautiful sister who's not afraid to take what she wants in life and love. . . . And this time she's in the game for herself and she is not holding back . . . or is she? The tall, dark, and sexy NBA star Phoenix Carter steps back into her life and takes her back to places she'd rather not revisit, no matter how good the lovin' was. . . . *Fourplay* is a story every man, woman, and sports fan will enjoy."

—Roxanne Jones, senior coordinating editor/VP, *ESPN The Magazine*

"Brenda Thomas is adept at capturing your attention and curiosity and then satisfying your appetite for more with compelling, believable and juicy drama."

—Curtis Bunn, author of *Baggage Check* and founder of the National Book Club Conference, Inc.

"Brenda Thomas proves to be a creative thinker, dazzling writer, and a captivating storyteller. She weaves an intoxicating—and sensually sizzling—storyline around Sasha Borianni that will have her fans reading the book while walking in traffic."

—Terry Shropshire, *Rolling Out Urbanstyle Weekly*

"You won't be able to put this one down and really won't want to."

—Troy Johnson, founder, AALBC.com

A Featured Alternate of Black Expressions Book Club

Fourplay

. . . the dance of sensuality

Brenda L. Thomas

POCKET BOOKS
New York London Toronto Sydney

POCKET BOOKS, a division of Simon & Schuster, Inc.
1230 Avenue of the Americas, New York, NY 10020

This book is a work of fiction. Names, characters, places and incidents are products of the author's imagination or are used fictitiously. Any resemblance to actual events or locales or persons, living or dead, is entirely coincidental.

Library of Congress Cataloging-in-Publication Data

Thomas, Brenda L., 1957-
Fourplay : the dance of sensuality / Brenda L. Thomas—
1st Pocket Books trade pbk. ed.
p. cm.
ISBN 0-7434-7727-8
1. African American women—Fiction. 2. Women in marketing—Fiction. I. Title.

PS3620.H625F68 2004
813'.6—dc22

2003069020

First Pocket Books trade paperback edition April 2004

10 9 8 7 6 5 4 3 2

Manufactured in the United States of America

For information about special discounts for bulk purchases, please contact Simon & Schuster Special Sales at 1-800-456-6798 or business@simonandschuster.com.

Mary C. Thomas

October 1925–May 2003

I miss you every moment.

ACKNOWLEDGMENTS

All praises to Allah, Most gracious, Most merciful.

I truly thank everyone for their love and support through all the challenges that faced me while these words trickled onto the pages. Special thanks to my family, friends, bookstores, book clubs, editor, agent, readers, media, fellow authors, and people who offered their business advice.

Mom, my tongue has forever been tied from calling out your name and my ears will never hear your response. It's only from my heart, late at night, that I speak to you, seeking your *advice* and sharing my accomplishments.

Dad, I thank you for my past and my present. My granddaughters, Jazzlyn, Briana, and Jada, you hold my future. I love you all.

Slow down, take your time, the road to the finish
is always more titillating than the finish itself.

—B. L. THOMAS

PROLOGUE

SASHA BORIANNI
Protector of Men
March 2003

Fine needles prickled my shoulders and moved down to my elbows. Moisture seeped from inside me and onto my thighs. Hot sweat gathered in my armpits. I felt like I was outside myself, looking in at the person having this experience. I could actually feel my head swelling with blood, and my pounding heart was surely about to come through my skin. Some force had been pulling me further and further away from myself. Part of me wanted to relax, let whatever was taking over have me, but I'd held on. How long had I been in this? Fifteen, twenty minutes, maybe? It always seemed longer than it actually was. I looked over at the clock: 6:00 A.M.

The sweat from my naked skin made me stick to the sheets. I eased my body farther under the comforter until it touched my chin. I longed to breathe in the cold air that blew in through my open bedroom window. But my cotton-dry mouth made it impossible for me to swallow. How would I get through this one? Use another one of my remedies? I'd been using them too often; it just didn't seem right to do it in the morning, even though I knew it would ease my personal trip.

My eyes took in the bedroom; the blank TV screen held my reflection, and the antique dresser where my collection of perfume bottles sat was a blur. Maybe my bed was too high off the floor, and that's why I felt like everything was in motion. I tried to focus my eyes and my thoughts.

Reluctantly, I eased one arm from under the covers and reached under the bed to where I'd kept the box hidden—from whom, I didn't know: nobody visited. I slid the box out and flipped through its contents without looking. Maybe I'd surprise myself by what I chose. Just the thought of it made my body relax. But no, it was too early. I should wait until later. Maybe tonight. Yes, definitely tonight.

PHOENIX CARTER

Another dead-ass hotel suite. They all looked the same at three o'clock in the morning, no matter what city I was in. I hadn't turned the television off, so I watched as highlights of the game we'd won replayed on ESPN.

My effort to get comfortable in the custom-made bed was useless. I gave up, rolled over, and headed to the bathroom. Relieving myself, I looked in the mirror over the toilet and wondered why the same people who had made my career were now trying to ruin it. On the television I heard the commentator ask, "Phoenix, is there any truth to the rumors about you recently winning three hundred grand at the poker table in Vegas?"

I'd done damn near everything over the last three years to clean up my image. I was no longer considered a thug. No more entourages of twenty deep. Shit, I was wearing three-thousand-dollar suits, but of course the media harassed me for that, always asking me how much they cost. And just because I'd picked up one little dirty habit, I was catching hell. I mean, I should've gotten some respect. I was twenty-eight, had been in the NBA for eight seasons, voted five times to the All Star team, had seven scoring titles and three championship rings, and made MVP countless times. Didn't they realize who I was?

Dragging myself back into the bedroom, I picked up her business card. I didn't even remember how I'd gotten it. Public Relations. Yeah, she'd been good at that, but Sasha Borianni had been good at a lot of things. I knew I'd need to call her after getting into LAX last night and having the press stick microphones in my face. Platinum Images. She wouldn't have that damn company if she hadn't worked for me. But I had to admit, right now I needed her ass.

LYOR TURRELL

I hated waiting for flights to take off, listening to the airline stewardess tell me how to escape—as if there actually were a way for me to save myself at thirty-five thousand feet in the air. I'm usually still not awake at six o'clock in the morning, much less able to figure out how to operate an air mask and what to do with the seat cushion.

It didn't help that I hadn't slept well the night before, so I summoned the stewardess. "Can you please bring me a black coffee with a shot of VSQ alongside it?" I asked, ignoring her surprise at my early-morning drink request.

Luck had definitely been on my side last night at Ari's art gallery opening when he introduced me to Sasha Borianni, the CEO of Platinum Images. She had been quite impressive, with those long legs and mouthwatering figure. I enjoyed the way her beautiful hand gripped mine in a firm handshake. Every time she moved, I'd catch just the slightest scent of her perfume. It was hard for me to concentrate. Sasha had a subtle sexuality that made me want to find out where it was coming from and, more importantly, why she was trying to hide it.

I'd studied her as she sipped and swirled a brandy snifter half filled with Hennessy Paradis. No apple or watermelon martinis for her. Listening to the way she described her company, it was evident that she was a woman with the ability to manipulate any situation she wanted. But more importantly, I watched and listened to what she was not saying.

During our brief conversation, I'd caught her looking at me, sizing me up like I could be a possibility. It was like that with black women; they were always cautious of crossing the color line. But when it came to money, it never mattered. I knew I had to be careful with Sasha because "sistas" were my weakness, and this time too much was at stake.

I'd never been in the habit of rushing business, but I

also could not afford to waste time. I reminded myself that Sasha's having worked for one of the country's wealthiest and most recognizable athletes would make her unimpressionable where money was concerned. I was certain her first instinct would be to protect her ex-employer, ex-lover, whatever the hell he had been, but I'd win her over. With the right amount of planning, Ms. Sasha Borianni would carry me on her back straight to Phoenix Carter.

SASHA

Pushing the box back under the bed, I turned over and hugged the pillow. I hated waking up feeling lonely, but I guess it was better than lowering my standards just to have a man to warm my bed. That's probably the other reason why I kept having these personal trips. I spent way too much time alone, thinking about the things I don't have in my life. But I couldn't deny that I enjoyed my antidote. It allowed me to slip away into my own private world.

In the past I'd tried a number of things—yoga, relaxation techniques, changing my diet, medicine, exercise—but nothing took it away. Ignoring it definitely hadn't worked. I didn't know what I was so damn anxious about anyway. The doctor said there was no physical cause for my panic attacks, that I was probably working too much. But no amount of rationalization had been able to rid me of what I preferred to call my personal trips.

It was probably last night that brought all this on. Freezing rain had been coming down all day, and I'd really wanted to stay home. But I'd agreed to attend Ari and Joan's art gallery opening.

"Lyor Turrell, international trader of many things, meet our friend Sasha Borianni, CEO of Platinum Images," Ari had said as I reached out to shake the hand of a handsome white man who stood about six-three and looked to be about forty years old.

"It's my pleasure," he'd said.

"Nice to meet you, Lie-or," I'd answered, curious about the foreign accent I'd detected.

"If you let your tongue roll off the roof of your mouth, you'd pronounce my name correctly. It's pronounced Lee-or."

"My apologies, *Lyor.* Did I get it correct that time?"

"I am sure there are not too many things you get wrong. Now, may I get you a drink?" he'd asked, as Ari excused himself.

"Yes, a Paradis, please." I'd turned and watched him stroll to the bar. He wore a black single-breasted, two-button suit that made him look like he'd just stepped off the runway in Milan.

He'd returned, handed me my glass, and took his seat beside me. I listened again for his accent when he spoke.

"Thank you. And what exactly do you trade, Lyor?" I asked, once again emphasizing the correct pronunciation of his name.

"As Ari said, I'm an international trader . . . of many things."

He quickly changed the subject back to me.

"What, may I ask, did you do prior to Platinum Images?"

I'd hesitated in answering, letting his voice linger in places where it shouldn't. "I provided executive services to Phoenix Carter."

Slowly he moved his head up and down. "I am quite familiar with Mr. Carter. I'm surprised we never met in that circle."

"What accent is it that I detect?"

Lyor paused, taking the time not only to decide on his answer but to let his gaze wander over my body.

"Israeli. I'm an Israeli Jew. If you would allow me the pleasure of your company, I'm sure I could offer you a business opportunity or two."

At that point, I should've told him that I didn't do white guys. But I was curious about his business, and I had to admit that he had struck a chord with me.

As if considering an intimate relationship with a white man wasn't enough, when I'd gotten home that night, I was surprised to find a message on my answering machine from a man I hadn't heard from in a long time. Phoenix Carter. I'd been reading tidbits about him on page 6 of the *New York Post.* According to the gossip column, Phoenix had picked up a taste for high-stakes gambling, and he'd been seen in some shady places. I'd assumed it wasn't a big deal, just something for the press to latch onto. But then again, maybe not.

PHOENIX

Lying across the bed, staring up at the ceiling, I realized that sometimes I hated being Phoenix Carter.

People, fans, always want what they think we have, but they have no idea how fucked up our lives really are. It was so much easier when I had less and my private life wasn't up for public scrutiny. I mean, what crime had I committed? So what, I'd bet on a few rounds of golf and played poker a few nights. And whose business was it if I liked to pass time hanging out at the tables in Atlantic City and Vegas? I mean, it was all in fun—or at least, it was until I'd played around and bet on the wrong thing.

Now Crystal's bitching about how we're gonna lose everything. How dare she threaten to take my kids outta school and go to her parents in Sarasota? I told her ass there was nothing to be worried about. But I knew better; too many details were coming out, which meant someone close to me was about to snitch.

I should've gotten in touch with Sasha months ago, at least to get my packages out of the safe in her house. But now I was left with no choice. She knew how to handle the press, the NBA, anybody who came up against me. I refused to call her again because I didn't want to sound desperate. But I was.

Thinking back on our relationship, she'd been good at everything, especially at pleasing me. I'd often had to stop myself from thinking about the last time I'd *really* been with her. I'd been walking out the door of her hotel room about three in the morning, after a wicked night of lovemaking, when I'd looked back and noticed her sheer, black panties, ripped and crumpled on the floor. And there was Sasha, lying on her stomach all sprawled out across the bed, whispering good night to me. Damn, she'd been good.

I picked up my cell from the nightstand and scanned through the numbers. But instead of calling Sasha, I found the number of a woman in Santa Monica who would immediately make herself available to me.

LYOR

First class had certainly changed. I looked around me at the young punks with their headphones turned up too loud, crying babies, and the woman polishing her nails. If I had not been so cautious, or as my family would say, economical, I would've purchased a private jet by now to take me wherever I needed to go. But all in good time.

Until then, I was forced to sit on a four-hour flight from Philadelphia to Dallas trying to score another deal while my mind was on Sasha Borianni. I called over the redheaded stewardess, whose heavy body soon would not be able to fit down the aisle, and ordered another VSQ, this time without the coffee. Reclining in my chair, I thought about what it would be like to be in Sasha's company. I pulled her card out of my pocket. But instead of concentrating on the business I intended to offer her, I could only think of the pleasure of having her long legs wrapped around me.

And as for Phoenix Carter, no matter how rich and famous he was, he would soon discover that the game he was playing wasn't on a level playing field.

SASHA

My first instinct had been to call Phoenix, but so far I'd resisted, even though the thought of him had me lying there thinking too hard about how it used to be. He hadn't mentioned anything personal in his message, but it was there, our sex, our memories, and I knew he felt it too by the way he kept pausing in his message. He'd left all his numbers, two-way pager, business cell, personal cell, office number, and private numbers at home.

Closing my eyes, I drew a deep breath, recalling the feel of his strong hands and how they'd roamed my body. I'd acquired an appetite for Phoenix's type of loving, which was something I hadn't been able to get anywhere else. Without thinking, I picked up the notepad where I'd scribbled his numbers and considered . . . Then the phone rang, bringing me back to the morning.

1

BEARING THE CROSS

"Sasha, hey, sorry to wake you but Pastor Price is about to be released from police custody."

"What? Bruce, what are you saying? Pastor Price?" Sitting up in bed, I recognized the voice of Bruce Reilly, lawyer to my client Pastor Nelson Price, a major figure among the Philadelphia clergy. He'd hired me to help position him in his run for president of the National Baptist Convention. I couldn't imagine what he could be in jail for.

Pulling myself out of my morning fog, I asked, "What happened? Was he involved in some sort of religious protest?"

"No, this is serious. His wife called the police early this morning, accusing him of domestic violence."

I was completely awake now, but confused as hell. This was unbelievable.

"Listen, he's being released on his own recognizance, and I'm taking him to his mother's. And just so you know, the press has already set up camp outside police headquarters."

Swinging my legs to the side of the bed, I looked on the nightstand for my remote, but it wasn't there. Instead I found it wrapped up in my comforter. I turned on *Good Day Philadelphia* to see if the news programs had begun to report anything.

"Bruce, can you get him out a rear entrance? And please tell him not to make any comments to the media. We both know how Pastor Price likes to run his mouth, but this is not the time for it. I'll meet the two of you at my office in an hour."

"All right. We'll see you then."

After hanging up, I realized that he probably had no idea that I'd already relocated my office. I began to dial Bruce's number, but then I remembered that Daddy had phoned last night, sounding a little intoxicated, saying he wanted to have breakfast with me. It wasn't unusual for him to buzz me late at night, but this request had been odd. He'd said it was important.

Before calling Bruce, I phoned Daddy.

"Morning, Daddy. Look, I know you wanted me to come by this morning, but I have a client being released from jail. Can I catch up with you later?"

"Slow down, busy lady, and yeah, I did see Pastor Price on television this morning. Those brothers are full of surprises, huh?"

"Yeah, I'm very surprised. Is it okay if I come over this afternoon?"

"Well, sweetness, any other time I would say okay, but

I need to talk to you. Do you think you could squeeze me in?"

Since Daddy always wanted me to put my business first, I realized I'd better hightail it to his house to see what was going on. "No problem, Daddy, I'll be there in about an hour."

I dialed Bruce's number, pushed our meeting back to 11:00, and gave him my new address. I then put a call in to my office, leaving a message for my assistant, Kendra, that I'd be meeting with Price and his lawyer at our new office at 11:00. I left a message for my partner, Michael Taylor, who I knew would be aggravated by the delay in our morning staff meeting, and asked him to start the meeting without me.

Damn, I hadn't wanted my day to start like this. I pushed Phoenix and my personal trips to the back of my head. I pulled on my robe and, walking out of the room, caught a glimpse of Pastor Price on TV being led from police headquarters to Bruce's black Mercedes.

Before heading to the bathroom, I pulled a pair of Seven jeans from a Bloomie's shopping bag and a white camisole with matching bra and panties from my dresser. I removed a white button-down shirt from its dry-cleaning plastic and threw everything on the bed. I took a few minutes to look over my ever-changing body in front of the full-length mirror that covered one wall of the bathroom. I'd gained a few pounds, but it just made me a fuller five-eleven. But what the hell? At my age I was supposed to show that I'd enjoyed life a little bit. I headed to the bathroom to quickly shower, and while brushing my teeth, I noticed that my hands were still shaky. I'd never taken the medication the doctor had prescribed for my panic attacks on a regular basis, so I turned on the faucet, filled my hands with water, and swallowed a Paxil. Maybe it would help today.

I was out of the house by seven-thirty. While waiting for my car to warm up, I checked the eight messages on my cell phone and the twelve messages on my office line. Couldn't life just slow down a little bit? I pulled into Dunkin Donuts for a decaf tea and a chocolate French cruller. It was no surprise when I crossed over Falls Bridge to West River Drive that I got caught up in rush-hour traffic. I tuned the radio to WJJZ and sipped my flat tea, trying my best to relax.

I turned onto Fifty-seventh and Girard. Daddy still lived in the same house in West Philly where I'd grown up. He'd managed to keep the house in pretty good shape and was always talking about selling it but probably never would. The house was too big for him by himself. That's why I was glad my son Owen and his family would be moving in to share the huge three-story, four-bedroom house.

I rang the bell and used my key at the same time. Stepping into the enclosed porch, I was overcome with nausea at the smell of pork bacon and burned toast that filled the house. I could hear Daddy talking, so I followed the direction of his voice.

Daddy was in the kitchen, talking on the phone to what was probably a woman, by the way he was smiling and whispering. I kissed his unshaved face. He put his hand over the mouthpiece and said, "Good morning, sweetness. Go sit down. I'll be right there."

Sitting at the dining room table, I looked around the room, which hadn't changed much, with its worn burgundy carpet and the chipped glass punch bowl that had been sitting on the buffet since my eighth-grade graduation. The living-room coffee table held a stack of newspapers and magazines, all of which had clippings of some media attention I'd garnered, either about my clients or interviews with me. Daddy was my biggest fan, determined that one day he would put all the clippings in a scrapbook. I made a mental note to hire a service to clean the house before Owen and Deirdre arrived.

Daddy shuffled into the dining room, wearing the brown tattered leather slippers he'd probably had over twenty years, along with his gray pajama bottoms that didn't match his blue sweatshirt. But hey, that was Daddy.

"You want some tea?" he asked, carrying an old grease-stained teapot.

"That's good." He set out two cups that held ginseng tea bags, which I'm sure somebody had told him was good for his blood. He shuffled back into the kitchen.

"What's this life-or-death reason that I had to be here this morning, and what the heck are you in there burning?"

Poking his head in the doorway, he said, "Your favorite: bacon."

"Yeah, right. Well, it stinks." My cell phone rang; I checked the caller ID, and when I didn't immediately recognize the number, I hit decline.

"That's what makes it so good," he replied. "You know you grew up on this stuff."

"Thank God for growing up."

He seated himself at the head of the table.

"So what's going on, Daddy?" I asked.

Looking in his cup rather than at me, he mumbled, "Well, I went to see Jerry the other day, and even though I'm not in any pain, he says I have cancer."

"Daddy, what the hell are you talking about? You can't have cancer. You just told me you had a checkup and that everything was fine." Nervously, I reached for the teacup, but my hand hit the rim, splattering its contents onto the table.

Grabbing a dish towel to soak up the tea, Daddy responded, "Look, baby, Jerry says he can get rid of it."

Dr. Jerry Gamble was a pinochle partner of Daddy's who'd been his personal physician over the years. He was like an uncle to me. "Daddy, Jerry isn't a damn specialist. He doesn't know everything!"

"Calm down, okay, and I'll explain. I went to see Jerry because I was having a problem, you know, going to the bathroom. Before I knew it, he was running tests and sticking a damn probe up my ass."

I had to laugh; I could only imagine how Daddy was probably cursing while having good ol' Jerry examine him.

"That shit ain't funny, Sasha. Your daddy ain't no damn gay blade."

"But cancer, Daddy? I mean . . ." I couldn't finish, because my words got caught in my throat.

Daddy noticed my trembling hands and covered them with his. "Where is the cancer, Daddy?" I managed to ask.

"Prostate, you know, under my balls. Where men get it," he answered, while ruining his tea with two heaping teaspoons of sugar.

"How do you know for sure? Have you seen an oncologist, urologist, or whoever it is men see for this stuff? I'm gonna make some calls and get you a specialist."

He took a piece of bacon, folded it between his burned toast, and attempted to answer me while chewing. "You don't . . . need . . . to go doing all that."

"Never mind, Daddy. What's Jerry's number?"

"I'm seeing him this morning, Sasha, and he wants you to come with me. Don't go getting worried, okay?"

"Daddy, how do you expect me not to be worried? You call me over here at seven-thirty in the morning and blurt out that you have prostate cancer." The sting of unexpected tears began to well at the bottom of my eyes, and I tried to turn my head to blink them back, but Daddy had already noticed.

He stood up and put his hand on my head. "Look, sweetness, I'm sorry to hit you with this, but listen, Jerry says they caught it in plenty of time, so I'm gonna be all right. Let me go upstairs and get my clothes on, and we'll get over to his office so you can hear it from him."

Not feeling confident that it was all that simple, I answered, "Whatever you say."

An hour later we arrived at Jerry's office inside the suites of the University of Pennsylvania Medical Center on Thirty-fourth and Walnut Streets. By then I was glad I'd taken the antidepressant, since my morning jitters had begun to subside. There were mostly women with children in the waiting area, and upon seeing us, the nurse came over to speak to Daddy as if he were there for a casual visit. He kissed her and the young blue-eyed blond receptionist on the cheek, referring to her as "baby" and "honey."

I couldn't imagine why this had happened to Daddy.

He'd always been so energetic and tough. He'd never had any heavy vices—a cigar once a night, a little Jack Daniels for the blood, and he'd always sworn they were what kept him young. Looking at Daddy I wondered what I would do if I lost him. Already, I'd lost my mother at birth.

I could tell by Daddy's casual attitude that he'd known about this cancer long before now. I picked up an old copy of *Men's Health* magazine and flipped through it, not reading, just looking at the pictures. After about twenty minutes, Jerry called us into his office.

"Hey, Doc," I mumbled, moving past the reception desk.

"Hello, Sasha," he responded, kissing me on the cheek. "Why so glum?"

"I shouldn't?" I asked, heading down the hall.

"Jerry, my man, what's going on?" Daddy asked as they shook hands.

Leading us into his office, Jerry placed his arm through mine and said, "Your daddy is gonna be all right, girl."

We took a seat in Jerry's small and cluttered office, and this time I didn't mince words. "Okay, Jerry, help me out here. What's this about Daddy having prostate cancer?"

"Like I told your father, he has a very high PSA reading, which probably means he's got a little prostate cancer."

"What the hell is a *little* cancer? That makes no sense, Jerry."

"What I mean is, we can probably shrink the cancer without even going into surgery."

"Okay, wait a minute, just help me understand. Exactly where is the prostate?"

"It's located behind the pubic bone and below the

bladder—it's about the size and shape of a walnut and produces seminal fluid, you know what I mean, right?"

"Jerry, look, just break it down for my daughter. It's up under my balls, where the sperm comes from."

"Okay, okay, I get it. Daddy, have you been having problems with your sexual performance?"

Jerry laughed while fiddling with his clipboard full of papers.

Stretching his legs out and crossing his feet at the ankles, Daddy answered, "Hell, no, I got one or two women I'm steady with. I was just having problems passing my water."

I still wasn't satisfied. "Are there still tests to make sure? And what about seeing a urologist?"

"We've run most of his tests. It doesn't appear that the cancer has spread outside the prostate gland. We've put him on medication to shrink it, and we'll retest him in a month for any changes. And if it makes you feel better, your father has already agreed to surgery if there's a problem, right, Joe? But believe me, your daddy will be fine."

By the time I dropped Daddy off, I was emotionally drained. I was already late for my ten o'clock appointment at Carson Savings & Loans. My cell phone had three new messages, but before listening to them, I called the office. Instead of the receptionist or Kendra, Michael answered. It was clearly a sign that things at the office were hectic.

"Platinum Images, Michael Taylor."

"Hey, Michael, what's up? Where's Kendra?"

"She's talking with the movers. She received your message and said to tell you that she took care of everything."

"Great. How are things at the office?"

"Out of control, of course, but I'm handling it," he said, clearing his throat. I realized he always did this when he was busy and felt I was bothering him. "I saw the story on Pastor Price. What the hell happened there?"

"Your guess is as good as mine. I'll find out when they get to the office. Is the move going that bad?"

Michael's voice went up an octave. "They have stuff everywhere, and you know I can't take disorganization but for so long. The movers claim they'll be done by six P.M. today. And they better be, or else it'll be reflected in their payment."

I thought about what a perfectionist Michael was—the movers were probably cursing him behind his back. Michael and I had met while he'd been director of marketing at a New York law firm. He had been looking to move back to Philly to be close to his family. He'd come on board just before I'd secured my first big account, and within a year I'd offered him a partnership. We worked well together because he was the total opposite of me. Michael's law firm experience and thoroughness drove me crazy. My view was to look at the big picture.

"Has Tiffany arrived in the office yet?" Tiffany, our senior PR specialist, had only been with us for six months. She had all the makings of a future partner. Before joining the firm, Tiffany put in two years as the marketing manager at a major advertising agency. She reminded me of my daughter-in-law, Deirdre, the way she mixed office savvy with street smarts. I figured her to be about twenty-six, but I had no idea what part of her heritage gave her her slanted eyes and straight hair. She carried herself as if she had no idea how beautiful she was.

"She's in the back, talking to the movers. We'll be taking the two consultants out to lunch, since this place won't be ready."

"Will you need me?"

"We'll be fine, Sasha. Here's Kendra. I guess she's finished flirting with the workers."

"Good morning, Sash," Kendra began, and without stopping to breathe she went through a litany of messages. "You have a message from John Worthington at Worthington Associates who wants to know if you're coming to the Jack and Jill Charity Ball, and two messages from the press."

I snapped out of my reverie. "Damn, about Pastor already."

"Seems like it."

"Anything from Lyor Turrell?"

"Nothing from him, but there was one from a very rude man. Mitchell, of Mitchell and Ness"—my hands tightened their grip on the steering wheel as I listened to Kendra—"who phoned, saying he and his client need to speak with you. However, I must say he was very reluctant to tell me who that client was. He even had the audacity to ask for your cell phone number."

"Shit!"

"What's that?"

"Nothing. Just something I need to take care of."

Maybe Phoenix's situation was more serious than I thought. Mitchell was Phoenix's lawyer. He was a partner at the law firm that helped launch my career as a personal assistant. "All right, I'll handle that when I get in."

"Okay, well, if that's it, I gotta go. Things are jumping here. Michael is on us to get this place in shape. Your desk finally came in, but your office is a mess."

As I turned onto Sixteenth and Race Streets, thoughts of Pastor Price and Phoenix Carter ran through my mind. I was still trying to take in the news that Pastor Price was a violent man. I don't know why I thought it was impossible. I mean, wasn't something seedy always being revealed about men of the cloth?

And as for Phoenix, the sound of his voice on my answering machine kept rewinding itself in my head. "Hello, Sasha, it's Phoenix . . . Phoenix Carter." As if another Phoenix would be calling me. "Uh, listen. I need to see you. I mean, we need to talk." The only thing he needed to see or talk to me about was getting his packages out of my house.

To distract myself from thoughts of Phoenix, I called my son, Owen, in California. I knew it was early there, but sometimes he was the best person to keep me grounded. I was so glad Owen and I had finally ironed out our differences. I didn't care what it took or what changes I had to make, I wasn't going to be one of those mothers who didn't talk to her son or vice versa. Deirdre, his wife, proved to have been my ally, and I attributed it to the fact that she'd married so young that she actually envied the fast life I'd led years ago. That's why I wasn't surprised by her excitement at moving to the East Coast. She hadn't lived anywhere else but Compton, so I hoped it wasn't going to be too much of an adjustment for her.

After four rings, Owen picked up.

"Hi, son, sorry to wake you."

"Yeah, hey, Ma, what's up?" he groggily responded.

"Look, your grandfather is having some health problems."

"Aw, shit. What is it?"

"Prostate cancer."

"Do you know how bad it is yet?"

Turning into the parking garage and taking my ticket from the machine, I held back tears. "They think it's just in that one area, so he's on some medicine to shrink the cancer."

"Well, don't worry. Deirdre and I will be there soon."

"I know."

"Ma, if anybody can beat cancer, Pop can. You know that, right?"

The sound of confidence in my son's deep voice was already making me feel better. "I know."

Shifting the car into park, I asked, "How's the packing going?"

"Good. Real good."

"And what about my grandkids?"

"They're excited, and they don't have a clue what's happening."

"I can't wait to see them. Well, I'm at my first appointment. I'll talk to you more about your grandfather tonight."

"Love you, Ma."

"Love you too, son."

At Carson Savings & Loans, I was supposed to review the final details for a business loan I'd finally allowed Ari Glassman, my business advisor, to convince me to get. I didn't expect the meeting to take more than thirty minutes.

Once inside Carson's, I strode past the teller windows to the customer service desk and told the representative I was there to see Joe Morgan, my loan officer. After making a brief call, she said, "I'm sorry, Mr. Morgan has been called into a meeting. In his place, Jordan Ashe, our branch manager, will assist you with your account." She led me to a small conference room opposite the service desk.

"Mr. Ashe will be with you in a moment," she said, leaving me in a room filled with pictures of people striving to do better, one of the themes of Carson Savings & Loans' public image. I poured myself a glass of water from the brown plastic pitcher on the credenza. I circled the table, choosing a seat facing the door so I wouldn't be surprised by whoever I was meeting with. I could hear the woman in the hallway telling someone that I was waiting. A few minutes later a tall, fair-skinned brother who looked to be in his mid-thirties filled the doorway.

"Sasha Borianni, I'm Jordan Ashe. My apologies that you had to wait," he said, placing my file on the table and reaching over to shake my hand. I easily noticed that his well-manicured fingers did not hold a wedding band.

"No, I'm the one who's late this morning. I'm sorry if it caused a problem with your schedule."

"No problem at all," he said, coming around the table toward me to take my coat and hang it behind the door. I quickly took inventory of his gray pin-striped suit and shirt cuffs that peeked out just a bit past the end of his jacket sleeve, revealing a hint of a monogram.

Instead of sitting across from me, he sat in the seat beside mine, allowing me not only to take in the smell of his cologne but also to check out his freshly polished wing-tip shoes and his slightly high-water pants.

Pulling his reading glasses from his inside jacket pocket, Jordan began, "I see here, *Mrs.* Borianni, that you were to bring an original copy of your business plan?"

I handed him the paperwork. He looked over the sheaf of papers that made up my file. Striking jet-black eyebrows that almost met at the center overshadowed his handsomely chiseled features. I noticed that his low cut, jet-black wavy hair didn't have a strand out of place.

I could tell by the way his bushy eyebrows went up while he reviewed my file that he was surprised by the amount of money I held in various financial institutions.

"Your numbers are quite impressive, *Mrs.* Borianni," he commented, once again putting emphasis on the *Mrs.* It was obvious that he was trying to flirt with me; the first page of my application clearly indicated that I was single.

"Thank you. I invested well."

"Exactly how long have you had Platinum Images?" Rocking back in his chair, he studied me. "And are you originally from Philadelphia?"

I wondered if he was going to keep asking me questions whose answers were already in my file. "Born and bred right here. And you?"

"Yes, I'm a Philadelphia kinda man."

He returned to his paperwork, and I wondered exactly what kind of man Jordan Ashe was, because he was definitely stalling.

"Well, *Mrs.* Borianni, it looks like everything is in order. If you could sign where indicated, please," he asked, offering me his gold Cross pen.

"You'll notice it's *Ms.* Borianni, just in case you missed that while you were looking over my file," I said. Without looking up I knew he was smiling.

"I'm sorry if I offended you."

"No need to be sorry."

"There is another question I'd like to ask."

I stopped writing, and when I looked up at him, our eyes met.

"I hear your firm is responsible for securing the Funeral Directors and Morticians Convention for Philadelphia next year. How'd you make that happen?"

"The mayor assisted me in securing that business. They'll be spending lots of money in our city."

"I hope Carson Savings & Loans gets a part of that business."

"That's a possibility. Why don't you attend Platinum Images' upcoming open house?"

"Certainly," he answered. "And who knows, maybe my bank—I mean, Carson Savings & Loans—could use a little PR."

"Really? Now, does that mean you're ready to stop being 'The Small Bank with the Big Heart'?" I couldn't stop myself from laughing at their slogan.

His bushy eyebrows went up. "You find that funny?"

I stood up and looked down at him, making him eye level with what he was probably really interested in.

"Well, Jordan, why don't I have my assistant give you a call to schedule a meeting at my office?"

"A meeting at your office would be just fine," he said, his gaze caressing my body. "Thank you for doing business with Carson Savings & Loans, Ms. Borianni."

2

COACHING

Driving up the Schuylkill Expressway toward Manayunk, I phoned my contacts at the *Daily News* and, more importantly, the *Tribune,* Philly's African-American newspaper, to see what they had on Pastor Price. I could only reach Christine at the *Daily News,* and I promised to give her the full story if she'd tell me what she'd heard, which didn't amount to anything.

I arrived at the new Platinum Images office on Main Street and parked behind the building in one of our designated spaces. The office was in a red brick building named L'Atelier, after the architect who designed it, and situated between two high-priced boutiques. Stepping into the lobby, I noticed Pastor and Bruce getting onto the elevator. Rather than catch up to them, I slowed down so I could ride the next elevator alone. I surveyed the building's lobby, soothed by its burgundy-and-gold interior and indoor waterfall. I walked over to the wall directory, where I could see, in little white letters, PLATINUM IMAGES, 4TH FLOOR.

Entering the heavy frosted-glass doors, I was met with the smell of varnish from the newly refinished hardwood floors. I leaned over the cherrywood reception desk to find loose wires dangling from the back of the computer and the telephone console lit up with messages.

To the left of the reception area sat a three-seat burnt sienna leather couch and two matching chairs, both still covered in plastic.

I could hear Kendra upstairs getting Pastor and Bruce situated. I made my way to the wide wrought-iron staircase and climbed the stairs to the second level. The first office at the top of the stairs was mine. It captured a view of what people in the area called the Manayunk Canal. The real luxury, though, was having my own full-size bathroom. That's what really sold me on the place. But it was time for business, so I walked down the hall past Tiffany's office to Michael's office. I knew before I got there that it would be immaculate.

Kendra greeted me in the doorway with a handful of messages, one of which was from Lyor Turrell.

"Sash, please tell me you haven't forgotten about picking up your new truck?"

I had, so I didn't answer, just shook my head and walked into Michael's office. As I expected, it was pristine. He'd opted for a rectangular glass table instead of the standard desk. His black flat-screen monitor sat on top of a Faghami credenza along the wall behind his desk. Opposite his desk were two red leather chairs where Pastor and Bruce were seated.

I hadn't seen Pastor since we'd returned from last month's trip to Nashville, where we'd attended the winter board meeting for the Baptist Convention. He'd been spectacular in his speech delivery, and we'd felt like we'd captured his seat. But with this problem in front of us, things could get complicated.

Sitting there, looking more haggard than holy, Pastor Price was dressed in a wrinkled navy blue crewneck sweater and jeans that told me he still hadn't been home. After greeting Pastor, I turned to Bruce, whose suits always looked like they were right off the rack at Sears. It was obvious from their expressions that I was about to hear a real sob story.

Before I could sit down, they both began talking at the same time. I let them ramble for a few minutes as I watched Pastor nervously pace the floor. Easing back in Michael's high-backed chair, I put my hand in the air and said, "Whoa. Why doesn't Pastor tell me what happened first?"

"Sasha my dear, it's not exactly something I'm proud of."

That was obvious by the way he faced the window, his back to us. I began to take notes; I knew I'd be hitting the button on a release to announce a press conference right after this meeting. It would have to be carefully worded to minimize the severity of Pastor's legal and domestic troubles.

"My wife and I had an argument last night. I finally confronted her with the fact that she's been having an affair." He turned to face me, pausing for my reaction. I gave him none. "Initially, Saundra tried to deny it, but I kept insisting that she tell me the truth. Finally, not only did she admit it, but she also felt the need to tell me that I was the reason she had committed adultery. She said I was boring. That all I cared about was my church." Nobody spoke as he paced the room, pondering the reasons for his wife's indiscretions.

Lowering his head, Pastor said softly, "I kinda lost my temper and slapped her."

I almost wanted to laugh at the thought of the classy, St. John-knit-suit–wearing Saundra Price getting slapped by her man of the cloth.

Bruce, who sat across from me, tapping his pencil eraser against his pant leg, spoke up. "You need to tell her the real problem."

I looked through the glass table at his scuffed brown shoes. Did this man have no sense of taste?

"Like any man, I demanded she get out of the house that my boring church had paid for. I told her I wasn't going to house her adulterous ways, and that's when she hit me with it."

"Hit you with what?" I asked, looking from Pastor to Bruce.

Bruce didn't wait for Pastor to respond. "This is it. When Pastor was in the seminary, to pay for his schooling he became involved with a loan shark who he later helped assist in making loans to other students."

Now it was getting interesting.

Pastor spoke up. "The real sin is that rather than stop when school was paid for, I continued and still have some loans out there to date."

"How big are the loans?"

"I think the biggest is about ten thousand dollars."

"To one person?

Pastor was pacing again. "Uh, some fellow ministers and some of our members."

"What's so wrong with that?"

"Sasha, you don't get it," Bruce added, glancing at his watch.

"Obviously not. Oh, wait a minute. Does any of this money belong to the church?"

"Yes, but not all of it. You see, Sasha, what makes it wrong is I charge people interest at seventy cents on the dollar, and the church doesn't see any of that profit."

I tried to break up the seriousness. "Maybe you should've been a banker rather than a pastor," I joked. Bruce was the only one who laughed. Pastor was engaged in his own thoughts.

"How did Mrs. Price come to call the cops?"

"She threatened that, if I tried to put her out of the house or the church, she would expose me to my congregation, the board of Baptist ministers, everyone." His voice cracked. "She'd ruin my ministry, my life."

"I see," I said, to his downcast eyes.

"I went after her. I didn't hit her again, I just grabbed her and started pushing her around, but I'm sure I scared her because I've never, ever displayed that kind of behavior. Believe me, Sasha, I am not an abusive man. When I finally let her go, she called the cops." Pastor sat down, his shoulders slumped, the picture of a broken man.

"Have you talked to her since they released you?" I asked, jotting a few notes.

"Of course, and she's very sorry. Saundra is more than willing to do whatever it takes to make things right, especially dropping the charges." He seemed satisfied with this, as if her dropping the charges would make everything okay.

I wondered, though, if that also meant she would give up her lover.

"All right, Pastor Price. Does anybody else know about the loan sharking, except those you've loaned money to?"

"Certainly not, and they wouldn't dare open their mouths. I gave those loans for good reasons. I helped to salvage people's homes and start children's college educations. They were all for a good cause."

"Are you sure your wife is behind you on this?"

"Sasha, believe me, my wife doesn't want to lose me or her status in the church."

"And have you spoken to the board yet?"

"They've scheduled a conference call for this afternoon at two o'clock."

"And what are you going to tell them?"

"Not the truth," he said, his gaze cast down in shame.

Bruce, who was uncomfortably shifting in his seat, spoke up. "The way I see it, as long as the loan-sharking doesn't get exposed, we can clean this up."

"This is how we'll handle it. I'll notify the media that you're holding a press conference at your church at five o'clock, just in time for the evening news. You need to make sure as many congregants as possible can be there, including the deacons, the deacons' aides, and whoever else you can gather up. We'll make it short and sweet, and I'll fax you the bullets you should read from. Understood?"

"Yes."

"And one more thing. I want Mrs. Price standing so close beside you that you two look like one person."

Once they left, I paged Kendra and asked her to come

back to Michael's office. Handing off my notes to her, I explained the situation, leaving out the details of the loan-sharking. While she sat behind Michael's desk, using his computer to quickly type up points for Pastor to read from, I sat opposite her in the chair, drafting a release that would be faxed to the media following the press conference. Pastor had credentials I could work with. He'd been in the ministry since he was twenty-three, had graduated valedictorian from high school and summa cum laude from college, and held a doctorate in ministry in addition to sitting on numerous civic and community boards in the city.

The next thing I had to handle was calling the Land Rover dealer in Cherry Hill, New Jersey. I was running too far behind to travel to Jersey, so I told them to deliver the truck, as they'd originally suggested. I was getting a deal on the truck from Ari, who was also part owner of the dealership. I'd met him and his wife, Joan, three years ago while on vacation in St. Lucia with my best friend Arshell. It was one of those times when we were trying to find ourselves, especially me.

Ari had been vacationing with his wife at their timeshare, and we'd noticed each other on the beach one afternoon. My initial instinct on encountering such a distinguished-looking man was to play his game—he'd look at me, I'd look at him, and we'd go back and forth until someone made a move. But when I remembered that the reason I was trying to "find myself" was a direct result of resigning from my position with Phoenix and ending a relationship with a man with whom I'd been engaged, I stopped playing the game.

Arshell and I kept running into Ari and Joan over the

next two days. Then one afternoon at lunch Ari approached our table and invited Arshell and me to a dinner party that he and Joan were hosting. Joan fit my idea of an older Jewish woman. She was about five-five, sixty years old, with salt-and-pepper hair, a ton of diamond jewelry, and plenty of misapplied makeup. They had a small but airy and richly furnished condo on the beach, and about twenty people had showed up for their party. Arshell and I didn't want to stay long because I wasn't in the mood for schmoozing, but Ari engaged me in conversation almost as soon as I arrived.

When he asked me what type of business I was in, I told him I was a public relations consultant. There was no way I was telling him I'd been somebody's personal assistant. Those few days on the beach had made me realize that I never wanted to work for anyone else again. I vowed that in owning my business, I would make my own decisions about whom I chose to take on as a client.

However, not even really knowing my situation, Ari began giving me advice on running a business, regardless of how small it was. He was the one who told me that I should get a loan if only because it would give me money to float rather than my own. He even offered to invest in my company so I wouldn't take a gamble, but I knew opening Platinum Images wouldn't be a gamble. I would make it—I didn't have a choice.

By four o'clock Kendra and I were pulling up in front of St. Jeremiah Baptist Church, where Pastor boasted a membership of almost two thousand.

I'd decided that it would be best to hold the press conference in the narthex so that the cameras could pick up the stained-glass cross inside the glass panels of the church doors. While Kendra went to get the media signed in and tell them where the press conference would be held, one of the deacons ushered me into Pastor's study.

"Good evening, Sasha," said Mrs. Price, her head held high, as if she had something to be proud of. Saundra was neatly dressed in a winter white coatdress with black button closures and a pair of black pumps. Her hair was freshly pressed and curled into a pageboy—I'm sure all in preparation for the television cameras. I was curious about the type of man she'd chosen to be her lover. Better yet, what type of man had chosen her?

But I was cordial. "Hello, Mrs. Price. Did you and Pastor have an opportunity to review the fax?" I hoped she sensed my distaste for the problem she'd created.

"We're ready," she answered.

"Mrs. Price, I wanted to ask you if you're still volunteering at Women in Transition?" I asked, catching her off guard.

"Occasionally."

"Good—we might need them, depending on how this progresses. Is Pastor ready?" I asked, looking around the study for some sign of him, just as he emerged from the bathroom, adjusting his tie.

"I see you've arrived, Sasha, my dear," he said, sounding far from the broken man who had sat in my office that morning.

"Pastor, how'd your conference call go with the board?"

"It went very well. They understand that things were taken out of context and have given me their full support."

"You lied to them, too?" Saundra asked.

I didn't have time for an argument, so I interjected, "If

the two of you are ready, I'd like to get started. The press has arrived, and we don't want to make them wait."

Saundra walked over and stood in front of Pastor, knotted his tie, and whispered something that I couldn't hear. Pastor frowned.

We emerged from his study and made our way to the narthex. There, Bruce stood to one side of Pastor and Saundra to the other while Kendra and I stayed behind the cameras. It was so easy to gather the media for bad news, but when there was good news, you had to drag them to a press conference. When the microphones went on and Pastor began to talk, Saundra moved closer to him, almost touching his cheek. I could tell by her quivering lips that she was just realizing the magnitude of the damage she'd done.

"My wife and I have come under a very stressful time in our marriage, as can happen in any marriage, and because this is a private family matter, it is our hope that the media and the public will understand and respect our family's need for privacy during this great misunderstanding. There is no doubt that my close friends and supporters are disappointed to hear these types of accusations, but I will ask your forgiveness, understanding, and prayers." Then, as if she'd rehearsed it, Saundra placed her hand inside her husband's. The cameras flashed.

Finishing his short speech, Pastor announced that he would take a few questions.

"Pastor Price, can you tell us exactly what happened last night?"

"At this point our lawyer has asked us—"

Before he could complete his answer, another reporter piped in, "Is it true you hit Mrs. Price?"

"I'll say it again. This has all been a misunderstanding. At no time did I strike my wife, and—"

Once again he was interrupted.

"You do understand that the court records will be open to the public."

"How will this charge affect your run for the Baptist Convention presidency?" questioned a different reporter.

I gave the nod to Bruce to step in. "I'm sorry, that's all the questions Pastor Price will answer. Thank you for your understanding."

By the time we concluded the press conference, it was six-thirty. Not only was I exhausted, but I was starved. I called in an order of food to Ms. Tootsie's, my favorite soul-food restaurant. Driving there, I phoned Daddy but got his answering machine. I wondered if things would go as smoothly as Jerry said they would. I'd heard that a lot of men went on to live full lives after having prostate cancer; I just prayed that Daddy would be one of them. I also tried to reach my friend Arshell at home, but her husband, Wayne, told me she was at the gym.

Once I was home and had eaten, I made myself comfortable on the couch, where I dialed Lyor's cell number. He picked up on the first ring.

"Hello, Ms. Borianni. I saw you this afternoon on television."

"I wonder how that happened. I wasn't in front of the camera."

"Maybe because you're so beautiful, they thought they'd throw you in to help the Pastor."

"The last thing he needs is for any woman besides his wife to be in a picture with him."

"Actually, it was a stock photo they'd run, saying that

in addition to his lawyer, he also had Philadelphia publicist Sasha Borianni of Platinum Images coaching him. Is that what you do? Coach men?"

"If they can afford to pay my price."

"Do you think Lyor Turrell can afford your price?"

"It depends on the services I'd have to provide." This man was really moving me. Aroused by the way his accent slipped off his tongue, I was slow to respond.

"No answer? Perhaps I could entice you by inviting you to ride with me to Myrtle Beach?"

He'd caught me off guard with that one. "Tonight? Well, I don't know, I have a lot of work, and I would have to pack, and—"

"No preparation needed; we'll get whatever you need when we arrive. The way I see it, we could charter a plane and get to know each other."

His offer did sound enticing. I could only imagine what we'd do alone in a chartered plane.

"Why don't I take a rain check on that ride?"

"Just know the ride is available whenever you're ready."

3

PLATINUM IMAGES

Before I could enjoy a full day at the office, I had to head off to an 8:00 A.M. breakfast at the Ritz Carlton on Broad Street, where I was the recipient of the Mayor's Excellence Award for the marketing campaign my firm created in the recent voter registration drive. The room held about two hundred people, mostly women. I sat there listening to my introduction, trying to remember if I'd cut my cell phone off, but before I could take a peek inside my purse, the host called my name and held her hand out for me to stand up.

". . . We thank her for her candidness, passion, dedication, and her willingness to help when we needed her. Ladies and gentlemen, I give you the CEO of Platinum Images, Ms. Sasha Borianni."

I wasn't long on words, just accepted my award graciously and vowed to do whatever I could to make

Philadelphia a city worth living in. But as I stood at the podium, I could've sworn I saw a familiar face in the back of the room. The face belonged to none other than Trent Russell.

Shortly after accepting my award, I headed toward the exit. From somewhere behind me I heard his voice.

"Sasha, did I miss you?"

I couldn't believe he was being so damn casual with me. Had he lost his mind? Just a few years ago we were engaged—that is, until he found out I was sleeping with Phoenix. He stood beside me.

"I . . . when . . . how'd you know I was here?" Damn it, why was I tongue-tied? I took a step backward.

"You didn't get the message that I'd called your office?"

What message? I thought, but answered, "Yes, I got the message, but I've been so busy I totally forgot."

"How are you? How'd it go in there? I didn't get to hear the whole thing."

I looked at his face, the teardrop birthmark under his eye, the outline of his growing beard. I had to get away from this man.

"It went well," I answered, tightening the grip on the award I held in my hand.

"Do you have a moment? I was hoping we'd have a chance to talk."

"Uh, no. I don't." I moved around him and pushed the button for the elevator.

"I thought we could catch up."

"Catch up? I suggest you call my office and schedule a meeting." I knew I sounded stupid, but the surprise of seeing him had caught me totally off guard.

"Your office?"

The elevator doors opened. I stepped in, turned to face him, and said, "You have a nice day, Trent."

As the elevator doors closed, I could hear him say, "I'll be in touch."

Trent was now a big-shot New Jersey politician. Why was he in Philly, and more importantly, why did he want to catch up with me? It was over between us; he'd made that very clear two years ago. I tried to remember what he'd had on—a black suit—no, maybe it was blue—cashmere coat on his arm. Yes, that was it. Damn, he looked good and he'd smelled good, too. Maybe I should've stayed and talked to him. I thought about going back upstairs, but then I'd look foolish. I didn't realize my cell phone was ringing or that the valet had pulled up in my raggedy car.

Rushing back to the office, I confronted Kendra. "Did you or the receptionist take a call from Trent Russell for me over the last few days?"

Fumbling through her call sheet, she said, "I don't see it on here, but I'll check. Is that okay? Are you all right?"

"No, it's not okay and I'm not all right. I ran into him today." Kendra could see that this was personal. "Forget it. From now on I'll answer my own phone. Where's Michael and Tiffany? Are they ready for our meeting?"

"Yes, everybody's here."

I'd scheduled a ten o'clock business strategy meeting with Michael and Tiffany. Once we all convened in the conference room, I gave Kendra the floor. My thoughts were on Trent.

"The responses have come in for the open house, so we should have at least 120 people in attendance. If you look on the sheet, you'll see I've broken it down into categories—media, clients, vendors, etc. We've gotten all positive responses on the direct mail pieces that went out for Worthington Associates. Also I need to remind you again to please"—her eyes scanned all three of us—"remember to update the client profiles when you speak to a client. The NFAMC is moving along. Our consultants have started the groundwork, securing the guest speakers, silent auction, and preregistration packets. I'm also working with the visitor's bureau to secure hotel and travel accommodations. Oh, yeah, and a Mr. Jordan Ashe from Carson's phoned to schedule a meeting."

She was nonstop. "Kendra, slow down." I must've spoken more sharply than I'd intended. Everyone looked at me as if I'd chopped her head off.

"I'm sorry, Sash," she said.

"Michael, Jordan Ashe will be yours. He's coming in to talk about some PR for his bank."

"No problem."

I had to calm down. I knew my attitude was stemming from my unexpected run-in with Trent.

Tiffany jumped in. "Well, in case anybody cares, I'm putting the final touches on the grand opening of Torre's Bed and Breakfast, which is scheduled to open after Easter. I've also received a signed contract from the new owners of the Uptown Theater."

"It's the same old shit, and I've about had my fill of all this multicultural diversity business," I said. "I want a piece of the business that these companies save for the white firms. Hell, we already lost the bid for that damn Constitution Center."

"C'mon, Sasha, don't start down that road again," Michael said.

"I mean, seriously, you watch, every time some damn group wants to hold a fundraiser or some shit to bring in black people, they'll be knocking on our door. I refuse to let Platinum Images be pigeonholed into only handling ethnic accounts. We might've lost our bid on the Constitution Center, but I refuse to lose out on the waterfront development project or anything else big that's coming up."

Pushing back her chair, Tiffany stood up. "With all that said, I guess we're done."

The one meeting I was seeking was with the Bowen Entertainment Group in Beverly Hills. I'd heard recently at a dinner party that they'd contacted the Philadelphia Film Office to begin plans for filming their next major motion picture in the Philadelphia area. The project wouldn't start until 2004, but if I wanted a piece of the action, I had to start my bidding now. Unfortunately, when I phoned Harry Bowen, I got no further than his secretary, who took my information and told me she'd have Mr. Bowen return my call.

At four o'clock Kendra walked into the conference room to tell me that the dealership had phoned, and my truck was being parked out front. I gathered my coat and purse and headed to the elevator, with Kendra on my heels. I was surprised by just how beautiful the Range Rover was, especially since this was the first time I'd seen it in the colors I'd selected.

"Sash, Sash, Sash, this truck is all that!" exclaimed an excited Kendra, walking around the truck's metallic white, gold, and chrome exterior.

Using the remote, I unlocked the doors. The new-car scent hit me. I ran my hand over the sand-colored leather seats, accented by jet-black piping. Why had I waited so long for this type of luxury?

"Sash, turn on some sounds. Here, I brought a CD down," Kendra said, leaning into the window.

It was time for me to go home anyway and get ready for the party, so I waved good-bye to Kendra, pushed in her Lil' Kim CD, and pulled into traffic. I was tickled by all the attention the Range Rover drew. Brothers nodded in my direction, and sisters slowed down to get a glimpse of who was driving, only to be disappointed to discover it was a woman behind the light-blue-tinted windows.

Inside the house, I threw my purse and coat across the kitchen chair and began sifting through the day's mail. The sounds of "Magic Stick" still rang in my ears as I danced across the kitchen floor. I noticed my telephone message light blinking. I pushed the speaker button and dialed into voice mail.

"Sasha, it's Daddy. I'm bringing a date to your party tonight, okay? So I'll see you later." I smiled, happy that he sounded good. The next message was from Arshell. "Hey, sweetie. Me and Wayne are on our way. I can't wait to see you!"

Shifting from one foot to the other while kicking off my shoes, I was scanning through utility bills and an offer for a Visa Platinum card when I heard another beep on the voice mail.

"It's Phoenix. Sasha, I'm waiting for your call." That was it, no hello, no good-bye. I was not about to be bothered with him this evening. I'd call him when I got good and ready.

Drying off after my shower, I moisturized my body from head to toe with Marc Jacobs lotion and two dabs of perfume. Removing my lingerie from its tissue, I put on a soft, black, lacy thong and matching demi-cut bra. In the bathroom I set my makeup case on the closed toilet lid and applied a little more makeup than usual, since I knew television cameras would be at the party.

I slipped into a clingy Narciso Rodriquez off-the-shoulder black silhouette dress that fell into a bias cut hem with a slight A-line. I'd carefully chosen a pair of three-inch Christian Louboutin heels that helped my garter belt and stockings all come together.

To top everything off, I was pulling out my good jewelry, which had been locked up in my safe for way too long. The safe wasn't very large, simply a 24-by-36-inch steel box that had been built into the rear of my bedroom closet. I tilted the nightstand on its side to retrieve the key from its hiding place.

Besides my jewelry and a small amount of cash, the only other thing I kept in the safe was Phoenix's three FedEx envelopes that he'd stashed there over two years ago. I already knew what their contents were, but I took a moment to peek inside one of the envelopes. Each one contained a black velvet bag that held about thirty diamond stones of various cuts, colors, and sizes. I wasn't attached to them, but I was sure they were probably the reason for Phoenix's phone calls.

From inside my jewelry box I retrieved my four-carat diamond stud earrings, a diamond solitaire necklace with eight round baguettes, and a platinum bezel bracelet—all gifts from Phoenix as an added bonus for being his lover while in his employ as his personal assistant. I was ready.

When I arrived at the office, I was impressed by Michael's decorating and even more pleased to see that not only were the *Philadelphia Daily News* and *Inquirer* present but also the *New York Post* and the *Philadelphia Business Journal.* The *Sunday Sun* was already snapping pictures of Tiffany and Kendra at the front desk. Michael quickly situated me in the conference room for a series of interviews.

As guests began to arrive, the place resembled a who's-who of the Philadelphia business community. Various clients came bearing gifts, ranging from flowers to chic office items that I knew Michael would turn up his nose at.

I didn't see Ari and Joan when they arrived, but they were there, too. Pastor Price had chosen not to come; we had agreed that for right now he should keep a low profile. Instead he had sent a beautiful arrangement of white roses and baby's breath.

I saw Jordan Ashe the moment he arrived. He stood talking with the mayor's press secretary, looking quite dapper in a dark brown suit that complemented his fair skin.

"Good evening, Jordan."

"Sasha Borianni, your beauty leaves me without words."

"Thank you, Jordan. Have you had an opportunity to look around?"

"I'd rather look at what's in front of me."

"My, aren't you being flirtatious tonight."

Our conversation was cut short when I heard someone ask, "Where's my girl at?"

Before I could turn around, Arshell was grabbing me around the waist. She and her husband Wayne had driven up from Maryland, where they lived with their three children. We'd both been so busy lately that all we'd managed to do was leave each other messages. I turned around and hugged and kissed both her and Wayne.

It wasn't hard for me to notice that Arshell was glowing and looked sexier than I'd ever seen her. She'd lost weight, maybe twenty pounds.

"I'm so glad you made it. Wayne, how are you? I think I've talked to you more lately than your wife."

"You're right. My wife has been making herself busy with everything and anything, it seems, to keep her out of the house," he said, attempting to grab Arshell's hand.

Wayne had on his standard IBM attire but had attempted to soften it up a little with a mock turtleneck. While Wayne went for a drink, I grabbed Arshell's hand and took her upstairs.

When Arshell stepped into my office, her face beamed with pride.

"Sasha, I'm so proud of you. You busted your butt to get here."

"I know, but I just didn't think I'd get here this fast. Enough about me. I wanna know what's been happening with you." I leaned against my desk.

"You know, the usual stuff," she answered, spinning around in one of the guest chairs.

"Are you still working part time?"

"Not really," she answered, tapping her foot to the music that filtered through the speakers.

"Then why have you been so damn busy lately?"

"I guess you could say I've found some other things to do."

It all sounded a little suspicious. "Arshell, don't bullshit me. What the hell do you have going on?" From downstairs I could hear Daddy's booming voice introducing himself to Tiffany.

"What I'm saying is, it's your night, so take your butt

downstairs. I need to make a quick phone call to check on the children."

I wasn't sure what she was so giddy about, but I liked seeing her happy because she was usually tired and burdened down with family stuff.

As I walked down the steps, looking at Daddy, it was clear to me from where I got my sense of style. I watched him remove his wool coat and hand his short-haired Borsalino hat to one of the waiters. He was wearing one of his favorite South Philly–tailored suits by Nanesco and matching black crocodile shoes. I made my way through the crowd to him.

"Hello, sweetness. You look like my baby tonight."

"Thanks, Daddy. How you feeling?" I asked, as he placed a dozen long-stemmed red roses in my arms.

"Stop worrying about me. Here, I want you to meet Clara. Clara, this is my daughter, Sasha."

Kendra walked past, taking the flowers from me.

Clara looked to be in her early sixties, her short, tightly curled hair dyed brown, probably to hide the gray. She was a little on the heavy side but nicely dressed in a black pantsuit.

"Hello, Clara."

"It's nice to meet you, Sasha. You've made your father a very proud man," she said, leaning in to kiss my cheek.

I looked at Daddy and said, "I want to show you around the place," but he interrupted, "You go 'head and do your thing. Me and Clara will get around."

Tiffany walked over to me and whispered, "Who the hell is that white boy over there?" There were quite a few white men in the room, so I didn't immediately know to whom she was referring. I followed her eyes and saw that it was Lyor Turrell. He saw me looking at him and started walking toward us.

"Good evening, Sasha," he said, taking my hand in his.

"Lyor, this is Tiffany. Tiffany, Lyor."

"Hello," he said, barely acknowledging her presence. Seeing that he'd totally disregarded her, she excused herself.

"I'm surprised to see you in town."

"That was the purpose," he said, now kissing my cheek. "You look exquisite." His eyes stared straight at my necklace.

"Thank you."

He moved in closer, his hands lightly fingering the baguettes on my neck. "These are very beautiful and, might I say, rare pieces."

"They were a gift."

"I'm not surprised," he responded, his fingers tracing my ear lobes and the diamonds they held.

Uncomfortable with the arousal I was feeling at his touch, I said, "I'm glad you were able to make it tonight. Can you stay for a while?"

Winking at me, he said, "I'm sorry, but I cannot. But you will still ride with me, won't you?"

"I haven't changed my mind."

By eight-thirty Michael was ushering everyone into the conference room for a champagne toast. He gave Daddy the microphone and positioned us at the front of the room. Before Daddy spoke, he grabbed my hand.

"Folks, I can't stand up here and give you some polished speech. I can only speak from my heart about this woman, my daughter, Sasha Borianni.

"Ever since she was a spoiled little girl, she's been the

spitting image of her mother—full of beauty, attitude, and class." He cleared his throat and continued. "She always wanted more out of life than life was willing to give. A few years ago, when she came to me, undecided about what to do with her career, my advice was, 'Do what you want, but know what you're doing.' So she created Platinum Images, and hot damn, she's been rolling ever since. Let me assure you folks that if you're doing business with a Borianni, then you're in good hands. I love you, baby, and I can't imagine my life without you."

I kissed him on the cheek. "Thank you, Daddy. I have everyone here to thank for their business, their support, and their encouragement—most importantly, my partner and staff. Without them I'd still be tucked away in the back bedroom of my home. So please eat, drink, and don't forget to pick up your mementos on the way out."

Just then I noticed Mitchell standing in the back of the room, involved in what looked like a verbal confrontation with Kendra. I had no idea why Phoenix's lawyer had showed up. Was Phoenix that desperate to speak with me? I quickly made my way to them.

I could hear Kendra getting riled up. "Yes, I know who you are. You're the rude gentleman that called the other day. However, I don't remember our sending you an invitation."

"I'm sure, young lady, if you ask your boss, you'll find out that I don't need an invitation," he answered, nodding in my direction.

Before I could respond, the editor from *Philadelphia Magazine* swooped in.

"Mitchell, how does it feel to have your former secretary achieve so much success?"

With a smile plastered across his face and his arm stiffly around my shoulders, Mitchell answered, "Well, little does she know, but I'm here in hopes that I can throw some exciting clients her way."

That was all I needed to hear to get my anxieties rising. There was no doubt that client was Phoenix Carter. I laughed, posed for a picture, and replied, "I can handle any client Mitchell & Ness throw my way."

I didn't want to be rude to my guests by going behind closed doors to speak with Mitchell, so I gave him a tour of the office as we talked.

"Were you ever going to return my call?" he asked, slipping his arm around my waist and heading up the staircase to the second level.

"I've been busy," I answered, hoping we could hurry and get this conversation over with.

He walked into my office and looked around. Standing behind my desk, he pretended to look at the pictures of my grandchildren on my credenza. "You've really moved up in the world from your days as a personal assistant, uh? This place must cost quite a bit."

"Mitchell, I have an office full of people," I said, from where I stood in the doorway.

"Phoenix doesn't want to hear that."

"Fortunately, I'm no longer on his payroll. He shouldn't expect me to drop everything just because he makes a damn phone call."

"That would be two phone calls from Phoenix and one from me. Sasha, I'm going to be perfectly frank with you. Phoenix needs you and this Platinum Images that you've set up," he said, looking around as if he despised what I'd accomplished.

Crossing my arms in front of my chest, I asked, "What can I possibly do for the great Phoenix Carter?"

Mitchell sauntered toward me, one hand stuffed in his pants pocket. "Let's hope it's more than what you did for him the last time."

"Good-night, Mitchell."

Back downstairs I caught up with Arshell and pulled her into a corner.

"You'll never believe who's been calling me."

"Phoenix."

"How'd you know?"

"I saw Mitchell come in, and you looked pissed. What the hell does he want?"

Before I could answer, Wayne walked up. "Honey, you ready?"

"Yes. Sasha, I'll give you a call this week."

I made it home before midnight and stripped down to my lingerie in the living room. I kept my jewelry on because its weight and beauty felt good against my skin. I poured a goblet of Moet and planted myself on the couch.

Having decided that I would call Phoenix in the morning, I turned my thoughts to the charming Lyor Turrell and tried to convince myself that he didn't turn me on. Taking another sip of Moet, I massaged my tired feet and gave some thought to Jordan Ashe. I was curious to see if he'd actually try to take our budding business relationship a step further. The one man I didn't want to think about was Trent and his sudden reappearance.

After channel surfing for a few minutes and attempting to watch a rerun of Eddie Murphy's *Trading Places,* I gave up. I clicked off the television, refilled my glass, and headed upstairs.

Setting my glass down on the already crowded nightstand, I switched on the lamp to locate my remote. This time I knew what to watch. Kneeling down, I pulled my goodie box from under the bed and chose my favorite movie. I inserted it into the player, threw back the comforter, and fluffed the pillows behind my head.

When I looked up, the images immediately captivated me. I settled in to see where these particular women would take me.

"I'm gonna take this slow for you," Jenna said, cradling her lover's head in her hands and pressing her full lips on her open mouth.

I picked up my glass and sipped the Moet.

With one hand Jenna fingered her lover's lips, while the other massaged her breast. She moved down and licked its nipple, back and forth.

Jenna placed her knees between her lover's thighs, opening them slightly, and reached down to touch her. Her lover's eyes closed, and she opened her mouth in anticipation of another kiss that never made it to her lips.

"I want to taste all of you," she whispered, moving from one nipple to the other. The camera did a close-up, and I could see Jenna's thumb massaging her lover's clit. "You're going to love me when this is over."

Not wanting to be left out, I slid down under the sheet and spread my legs, touching my own pulsating clitoris. I would've never imagined that my body would respond with such lust to these women's lovemaking.

Jenna teased, kissing the inside of her lover's thighs until her lover pleaded.

The sounds no longer came from the television but out of my own mouth. I looked down to find my two fingers gliding along my own moistness. The camera closed in tighter. Her lover thrust her body against Jenna's hungry mouth, which took long laps of her waiting orgasm.

Waves of heat cascaded through me. My insides throbbed. I pushed now, three fingers, deep inside myself, until the wet slickness of the motion inflamed me. I was desperate to find that spot that would relieve me.

"Come for me," Jenna told her lover.

"Ohhh," I moaned, as my own juices poured onto my fingers. I was coming, they were coming, our bodies moved in unison.

Emptied of all my anxieties and satisfied that I'd taken myself to that special place, I turned onto my side, pulled the comforter to my shoulders, and drifted off to sleep.

4

PHOENIX RISING

April

Over the next few weeks Platinum Images began receiving significant press as a result of the open house. Our phones lines were constantly busy with calls from prospective clients.

I was on the phone with Pastor Price, discussing his recent meeting with the church's executive board, when Tiffany walked in and turned the television to Comcast Sports. "Sasha, you might want to see this."

The shot was of Phoenix coming through the Philadelphia airport, swamped by reporters who were questioning him about his gambling. I could see the frustration on his face as he made an attempt to ignore them. Finally the team spokesperson jumped in to defuse the situation.

"Mr. Carter will not be taking any questions this afternoon. We're on a tight schedule. Thank you."

"What's the reason he's not answering them?" Tiffany asked.

"I can't figure him out—first he leaves me a message with all his damn numbers, his lawyer visits, and then nothing."

"Well, I'm off to meet with a client. I'll talk to you later."

"Thanks. Hey, you want to have dinner one night this week?"

"Sure."

Rather than be concerned about Phoenix, I headed downstairs so I could greet Jordan Ashe prior to his eleven o'clock appointment with Michael. I met him just as he was about to enter the conference room.

"Welcome to Platinum Images, Jordan," I said, extending my hand, which he held in his longer than necessary.

"Nice to see you again, Sasha."

"You too, Jordan. I'm glad you were able to keep the appointment. Can I get you anything?"

"Only if I can have what I see standing in front of me."

"Now, Mr. Ashe, I thought you were here on business."

"You've already told me that your partner would be handling my account, so that leaves me to assume that you might be open to dinner."

"Dating clients isn't such good business practice."

"Does that mean I'm getting passed on like Jell-O in the buffet line?"

I laughed at his corny line. "No, Jordan. Where would you like to have dinner?"

"Why not let it be a surprise? I'll pick you up Sunday evening?"

"I'll see you then."

By midafternoon the office had quieted down, so I decided to skip out early. I'd left another message for Harry Bowen and picked up my purse to leave when Kendra stepped into my office with a suspicious grin spread across her face.

"I think you have an unexpected appointment."

"You think? I thought it was your job to keep my schedule." Before she could give me a name, in strolled Phoenix Carter.

My heart beat rapidly against my chest. "This is a surprise, Phoenix. What brings you to Philly?" I asked, pissed that he was still able to make me feel that way.

He closed the door behind him and stood in front of my desk, making me look up at him. It was obvious he too was hesitant about getting close to me, as there were no handshakes or kisses.

"You forget I play basketball."

"And a lot of other things, from what I saw this morning on the news," I said, in response to his sarcasm.

"You heard right."

I wanted to check myself, look in the mirror, make sure I looked my best. "What brings you here to Platinum Images?"

"Obviously you weren't concerned, since you didn't return my phone calls," he said, tapping his fingers on my desk.

He looked around the office, then back at me, which gave me a few seconds to take him in. Gone were the baggy jeans, wife beater, and long platinum chains with his number attached. A soft gray designer suit draped his long muscular body. No man could wear a suit like Phoenix Carter. His jewelry was simple—a platinum and diamond hoop earring in one ear and a brilliant diamond bracelet dangling from his wrist. Even though the media was always writing that he was a more mature athlete, his cool demeanor told me that he was still hiding a part of him that I was very familiar with.

I looked at him dead on, determined not to let what I was feeling between my legs stop me from thinking clearly. He backed up and sat on the couch.

"And so, you were giving me an excuse as to why you hadn't responded to my calls yet."

Stacking the papers on my desk, I replied, "I've been busy. As a matter of fact, I believe my assistant left a message at your office."

Under my desk, I squeezed my thighs together, hoping to stop the throbbing his presence caused. A few years ago I would've closed my doors and had him right there in my office. I was determined to have more restraint now.

"You should know me well enough to know that I wouldn't respond to anybody but you."

I pushed my chair back from the desk and stood up. Even though he was at least ten feet away from me, I was suffocating in his presence. I opened the office door. Glancing over the balcony, I spotted his small entourage. Some things never change. I waved to his bodyguard, Trey. There was another well-dressed brother and a white woman who looked like a Victoria's Secret model. To other people she might have appeared to be with one of his friends, but experience had taught me that she was with Phoenix. That's the way it went in the great underbelly of sports. Many times in the past Phoenix and I had argued about why black athletes date white women. His reasoning had been that black women run their mouths too much. They weren't patient enough to wait and see what's in it for them. White women do things more strategically, he'd said. More importantly, they keep their mouths shut. I thought differently.

I turned around to find Phoenix had settled comfortably on the couch, his long legs stretched out in front of him and his hands laced behind his bald head.

"Why don't you come sit next to me so we can talk more privately?" he asked, patting the seat cushion.

I chose instead to sit in the chair across from him.

"What do you want?" I asked, hoping it wasn't me.

He laughed, pulled back his sleeve to check the time on his diamond bezel watch. "Something I haven't had in a long time."

The intercom on my phone buzzed, and I rose from the chair, glad for the interruption. I walked over to the credenza and picked up the receiver. The receptionist said, "I'm sorry, Sasha, but you said you wanted to talk to Mr. Turrell when he called."

Damn, I'd been waiting for him to call, but there was no way I could talk to him now.

"Can you please tell him I'm in a meeting and get a number, so I can return his call?"

Annoyed by Phoenix's presence and that he'd caused me to miss Lyor's call, I snapped out of my sensual reverie. "Okay, Phoenix, spit it out. What did you come for?"

"I've come for you, Sasha."

"Don't waste my time."

"I want you to come work for me and put a lid on these gambling rumors."

"If they're rumors, then why hire Platinum Images? Gambling *is* legal in some states."

"Weren't you the one who told me that contrived accusations can kill a career?"

"Are they contrived, or is throwing your money away how you get your thrills now?"

"I'm sure you of all people haven't forgotten how I get my thrills." He paused, licking his lips. "Sasha, seriously, I need you to put a lid on this shit."

"A lid on what? That you play poker till the wee hours in your hotel suite and that you were recently spotted in Atlantic City the night before the loss to New York?"

"I see you've been keeping up."

"My job is to watch the media, and you just happen to show up in it lately."

"You with me or not?"

Before answering, I sat on the arm of the couch opposite him, crossing my legs. "I can't afford to get involved with you again, Phoenix."

"We don't have to be involved. Not unless that's what *you* want. What I'm offering is for you and this firm to make a lot of money."

"I'll have to discuss it with my partner and get back to you."

He stood up, adjusted his suit jacket, and calmly said, "Fuck a partner. I'm your partner on this one. Listen, Sasha, I can't get into the details, but somebody obviously has it in for me, and if the shit doesn't stop soon, I could be in some serious trouble. Are you with me or not?"

The room was silent as he waited for me to answer.

"What do I get out of this?" I asked, having to look up at his towering body.

"You've always named your price before."

"Give me a few days to see what I can pull together."

He stepped closer into my space. "You won't regret it," he said, then kissed me on the cheek and walked out the door.

I slid down onto the couch and took a deep breath. I heard Kendra running up the stairs.

"Sash, I'm sorry, but it wasn't like I could stop him. He's Phoenix Carter."

"I know. Sit down for a minute, I need you to do something for me."

"You're not mad?"

"No, it's all right. I want you to pull up everything you can find on him, especially everything that's being said about his gambling. Go on the Internet and print out everything. Also, call Burrell's news clipping service and get them to do some research for us. Have them go back about a year and see what they can turn up."

"Are you going to work for him again?"

"How'd you know about that?"

"Everybody knows about you and Phoenix."

"We'll see if he can come up with the monthly retainer first."

"Right, like that'll be a problem."

It was after seven o'clock when I was finally ready to leave the office. I'd pulled up several boilerplate contracts to compose one for Phoenix, but nothing seemed to work. I phoned Tiffany and Michael for a quick conference call. I told them about my conversation with Phoenix and his request to retain our services.

Tiffany was eager. "I say let's do it. The business would be great for us."

"But Phoenix is very demanding, and he'll try to dominate our time, mostly my time."

"Then the boy's gotta pay for it," Michael said.

"That's my point; how much do we wanna charge him?" I asked both of them.

"Why not hit him for two hundred and fifty thousand dollars for twelve months, plus expenses?" Michael suggested.

"Not bad, Michael. Why don't you work the numbers, and Sasha and I can put together the contract in the morning."

Before going home, I returned Lyor's call and left a message. I also phoned Trent, who'd also left a message that I had yet to return.

"Hi, Trent. It's Sasha."

"You don't have to identify yourself. I know that voice. I'm glad you called. How are you?"

"I'm good."

"How's your family? I already see business is good."

"Thanks, and my family is fine, but . . ."

"But why am I calling?"

"Yes."

"I'd really like to see you, and since I'll be attending the mayor's fundraiser that your firm has organized, I was hoping we could spend some time together. You know, like I said before, catch up."

All of me wanted to say yes, quickly, before he changed his mind or remembered how I'd hurt him, but I didn't want to fool myself.

"Sure, Trent, call my office when you get to town, and I'll see if I can fit you in."

5

OLDIES BUT GOODIES

Sunday evening around five o'clock Jordan showed up behind the wheel of a not so new, but very well maintained, dark blue BMW 735I. I was glad to see he was dressed casually in a brown sport jacket, tan V-neck sweater, and brown pants. He'd topped it off with a pair of brown kidskin leather shoes. I wasn't sure where we'd be going, but I'd wanted to be dressed appropriately, so under my silk pashmina I wore a simple black short-sleeved, ankle-length Prada knit dress. At first glance it appeared to be see-through, but the only thing visible was the body-fitting camisole slip I wore underneath.

Jordan was the perfect gentleman, opening the car door and making sure I was comfortable. His car smelled of the vanilla-scented tree he had hanging from his rearview mirror. He'd chosen to play *One Last Cry,* an outdated Brian McKnight CD. He complimented Michael's work with the bank. Then he asked, "Would you mind if we stopped at my house for a drink, since our reservations at Buddakon aren't until seven-thirty?"

"Not at all. I'm following your lead tonight," I replied, trying to sound enthused.

We drove into Old City and parked on a quiet, tree-lined street. Stepping inside Jordan's house, I felt like I was at the African-American History Museum. His walls were adorned with sculptures and prints, and an Egyptian mud cloth was draped over the back of the couch. He gave me a tour upstairs, where he had a guest bedroom and home office. His bedroom was decorated in a blue that made me think I'd stepped into the ocean.

Returning to the living room, he offered me a drink from what he referred to as a gentleman's wine cellar. Opening the basement door, he motioned for me to follow him.

In his basement were three wine storage units that to me simply resembled mini refrigerators, but he said they'd cost him almost $1,000. He selected a bottle of Chateau d'Yquem, Sauternes.

We returned upstairs to the dining room, and he began to explain his passion for wine. "The important thing when opening a bottle of wine is to be careful of the way the cork slides out," he said, lifting a silver corkscrew from its boxed holder.

Although I was listening halfheartedly, his voice was creating a tingly feeling in me that caused my nipples to perk up.

With his eyes on my breasts, he commented, "It looks like you're enjoying your wine lesson."

"It's either that or the person who's giving the lesson," I replied, wishing he would reach over and squeeze one of them.

He continued. "If it slides out too easily, then it's probably rotted, which means air has gotten into the bottle and spoiled the wine." He pressed the tip of the corkscrew into the cork, twisted it out of the bottle's neck, and waved it under my nose. "Tell me how it smells. If it's vinegary or musty, then I'll pour it down the drain."

"Is that how you men do us? If a woman smells vinegary, then you throw her away?"

Ignoring my comment, he placed one of the glasses he'd set out in my hand, his eyes locked with mine. "You'll notice that I don't do fancy wineglasses with all those cuts and flowers and stuff. I prefer a clear ovoid bowl with a three-inch stem that holds about ten ounces."

I wanted to ask what the hell *ovoid* was, but instead I pursed my lips and nodded my head. He stood to the side of me, placed his hand over mine, and corrected my hold on the glass.

"Since your hands can affect the wine's temperature, you should always grasp the stem and never the bowl."

"I see."

"Then you tilt the glass sideways, like so."

He poured my glass half full and then his. "You should watch for color, which means you should try to hold it against something white."

He was going a little overboard for me, but it was intriguing to see how passionate he was about his wine. I wondered what I had a passion for besides work.

"You see, Sasha, what you're looking for in a white

wine is clearness. Brown tinges would mean that the wine is dead."

"What color do you look for in a woman, Jordan?"

"You're about the color of coffee with two creams, correct? That would be my choice."

"Good answer."

Placing the glass to my lips, I said, "I'm ready for a taste."

"Okay, but just a sip, or maybe"—he eased the glass away from my lips—"maybe I should make you beg."

I sipped the wine. "Sasha Borianni doesn't beg for anything."

"I want you to gently work the wine inside your cheeks with your tongue, then swallow. Slowly."

"Mmmm."

I'd already swallowed my wine twice and Jordan was still holding his inside his cheeks. When he finally swallowed, he asked, "What do you think?"

"Either I just had an orgasm, or this stuff is really good."

He almost spit out his wine laughing.

After finishing the bottle, we walked to Buddakon for dinner. The maître 'd greeted Jordan with familiarity, so I assumed he was a regular. The entrance had a twenty-foot-high gilded Buddha statue, and along the left wall was a waterfall. We were seated immediately, and while Jordan tasted and selected wine, I took in the restaurant's ambience.

Over dinner I learned that Jordan had been born and reared in the suburbs of Philly. He'd received both his bachelor's and master's degrees from Morehouse in Atlanta. Jordan had never been married and had no children. A perfect catch.

When the food arrived, he named all the items: garlic grilled shrimp with long-life noodles, Szechuan-crusted tuna with wasabi sour cream, and Japanese gnocchi. He wanted me to taste everything and fed me with his chopsticks. Either I was a little high from all the wine we'd been drinking, or Jordan was a long way from the brother I'd met at the bank.

After spending two hours at Buddakon and feeling like a Buddha from all the food I'd eaten, Jordan asked me if I liked oldies. We took a cab to Eighth and Callowhill Streets to Beyond Nightclub. I was excited about getting a chance to hang out. It wasn't that I didn't get out, but most of my social events were business.

Beyond was a remodeled warehouse with two large rooms, three bars, and different music on both sides. The place was crowded with an over-thirty group, but what intrigued me most were the fashions people had held onto.

The men wore two-toned alligator shoes with tassels and buckles, a ring on every finger, and big-brimmed hats with feathers. Every man over forty-five had a toothpick hanging from his mouth. The women mostly wore red, and shapes didn't matter because everything was tight, with breasts and love handles bulging. But everybody was happy—it was like a reprieve from your daily fast-paced life. A chance to go back in time, do the old dances, wear the old clothes.

We found a space to stand at the bar, and when the Temptations started singing "The Way You Do the Things You Do," I pulled Jordan onto the dance floor, and my stuffy banker began to move his ass like a real brother. We stayed on the floor for two records straight, and after dancing through the extended version of James Brown's "Get Up offa That Thing," Jordan's yellow face turned pink and even his hair was out of place.

By midnight Jordan and I were both exhausted and decided to call it a night. We returned by cab to his house, where I was reluctant to have him drive me home. But being the gentleman that he was, he insisted. I convinced myself that this probably wasn't the first time he'd driven intoxicated, so I strapped on the seat belt and rode with him along Lincoln Drive, hoping the cool April breeze would clear my head.

I toyed with the idea of inviting him inside as he walked me to my front porch.

"Jordan, I really had a good time tonight. Thanks so much for getting me out of the house."

"This won't be the last time, especially with the way you were moving on the dance floor."

"Are you going to be all right to drive home?"

"Yeah, I'm just a little high, that's all. Not unless you're going to let me sleep on your couch."

I pulled my keys out of my purse and unlocked the door.

"I take that as a no."

I planted a kiss on his wine-flavored lips and said, "Good night, Jordan Ashe."

Even though I'd let Jordan leave, it didn't negate the fact that I still didn't want to be alone. I was horny and hadn't been with a man in two months. There was no use in dwelling on what I didn't have, so I opted for a hot bath. I undressed, while the tub filled with water and Dirty Girl bubbles. Without thinking of the consequences, I called the one man who I knew had always been able to satisfy me.

There was loud music and people talking in the background, so I knew he wasn't alone.

"Sasha, baby, what's up?" Phoenix asked, not the least bit surprised to hear my voice at one o'clock in the morning.

I tried to think of a quick lie. "I've come up with some ideas that I thought might work for you," I said, slipping into the bubble-filled tub. I knew he could tell I wanted more than that.

"Is that all you wanted, Sasha?" he asked, then yelled at someone to turn the music down.

Maybe it was just me, but why did he have to keep saying my name the way he used to when we'd made love? "Yes, but it sounds like you're busy."

"Shit, Sasha. You know I'm never too busy for you. Where are you?"

"Home."

"Perfect, now why don't you let me fly you up here to Toronto so you can tell me in person what you can do for me."

That's when I came to my senses and realized who I was talking to—a man who could actually fly me to him at any hour of the night.

"Look, Phoenix, I have to go."

By the time I dried off, I knew that I didn't want to watch DVDs or anything else that reminded me that I was by myself. I thought of calling Jordan, but he was probably already sleeping. I thought about other men I knew whom I could possibly call to give me what I needed.

Naked, I went downstairs, rifled through my purse for my Blackberry, and looked up a number. I'd met Coach, as I'd referred to him because of his position as head basketball coach at one of the local universities, when I was still working for Phoenix. Most of the time he lived alone, or so he said, but right now that didn't matter. I gave him a call on his cell. He answered, was glad to hear from me, and arrived at my house within the hour.

6

POSTURING

With Tiffany's help, I reviewed the file Kendra had compiled on Phoenix. There was no hiding the fact that Phoenix had become a high-stakes gambler. What I couldn't understand was, if he gambled in public places, why was it necessary for some of the papers to link their information to an anonymous source? Hell, it seemed to be common knowledge.

Tiffany suggested we separate everything into two piles, one with just the regular humdrum rumors and the other with articles that mentioned that there was more to it. We reviewed them separately, both noting that there was some mention of golf at $50K a hole and private poker games. The most obvious one was a reporter who was hinting that Phoenix was possibly betting on NBA games. Tiffany agreed that there was something that

Phoenix wasn't telling me. I was determined to find out what that was during my meeting with him in New York that afternoon.

I knew Phoenix wasn't hurting for money. His annual income topped $60 million, including the many endorsements deals he'd secured. Carter Enterprises had earned $100 million last year alone. All of that could easily be threatened if his image was tarnished, but it would take more than hearsay for that to happen. Having been close to Phoenix, I also understood that the money came in second place to his reputation and popularity. That's where I came in.

Before leaving for New York, I had a meeting with Pastor Price and Bruce to discuss the negative publicity of Mrs. Price's battery accusations. Pastor told me that he and Saundra were still together, at least in the eyes of his congregation, but they'd moved into separate bedrooms.

"Pastor, I've been contacted by Women Against Abuse and the Pennsylvania Coalition for Battered Women. They are teaming up to protest outside your hearing next month."

"What the hell does that mean? The charges have been dropped." Pastor looked from me to Bruce.

"This is my suggestion. Since Mrs. Price is a volunteer for Women in Transition, I think she should allow herself to be interviewed by a reporter that I select. She can reveal that the two of you had an argument, as any married couple does, and that because of her work with battered women, she'd panicked and called the police. She can emphasize to the reporter that you did not put your hands on her."

"Bruce, what do you think?" Pastor asked.

"Sasha is right."

There had been no further mention of the loan-sharking. Pastor had closed down his operation and was personally donating, or so his congregants thought, ten thousand dollars to their Christian school fund.

While I was en route to the train station for my trip to New York, Lyor called my cell phone.

"Hey, Lyor. I see you still haven't made it back to Philly."

"I am rather close by."

"That could mean New Jersey, New York, Delaware."

"New York."

"Really? I'm on my way up there to meet with a client."

"Why not meet with me, too?"

I knew that Phoenix had a game that evening. "I don't know what your schedule is, but I won't be finished with my client until about five o'clock."

"I'm here for the night, so just give me a call, and we can have dinner, share a drink, whatever you'd like."

Feeling a little guilty for making plans to see Lyor, I decided to give Jordan a call. I was beginning to like him, and we both had joked about the possibility of our being Philly's next power couple.

"Hey, is this my Philly Cream Cheese?" Jordan joked at a nickname he'd given me.

"I hope so. Are you busy?"

"I have about half a minute before I head off to a meeting. Where are you?"

"I'm on my way to New York to meet with a client."

"Aww, I was hoping we could get together tonight."

"I'm sorry, but I probably won't be back until late. What about tomorrow?"

"Not good—I'm attending my first Blue Cross board

meeting. Listen, I gotta run. Call me when you get in tonight."

I arrived in New York at one o'clock in the afternoon, and a limo was waiting for me at Penn Station. The driver had been instructed to take me to Lloyd's Gym on the Upper East Side, where Phoenix was working out.

I entered the empty gym, went upstairs to the second floor, and wandered around until I found Phoenix in the weight room, finishing up his workout. I watched from the doorway. He lay on a weight bench, his legs spread apart, lifting what looked to be over 200 pounds. The muscles in his arms and thighs flexed as he gripped and lifted the bar over his head. On his fourth set of reps, sweat slid from his body onto the floor. I turned away.

He rose to a sitting position and wiped the sweat from his face with a towel. Involuntarily my eyes took in his many tattoos.

"Sasha, what's up?" he said, sweat clinging to his naked chest. When he stood up, I noticed that he had more muscle than when I'd last seen him shirtless. He walked toward the door marked "Men's Locker."

"C'mon," he said, gesturing for me to follow him.

"I can't come in there. I'll wait."

"You're kidding, right?"

I relented and silently followed him into the locker room.

While he showered, I sat on a bench in front of his locker. It had been a long time since I'd been in a men's locker room, where the musty scent of dirty socks and Gold Bond powder filled my nostrils.

Phoenix stepped out of the shower, the towel wrapped around his waist barely covering him. This was not good.

He rifled through his Nike gym bag, pulled out his shoe bag, then removed his suit from the Louis Vuitton garment bag that hung outside his locker.

I watched as he applied deodorant and slapped after-shave onto his face and bald head. Neither one of us said anything, and when the silence became unbearable, I spoke up. "I've been reviewing your file, and I have some questions I need to ask you. I can't figure out . . ." I trailed off, distracted by Phoenix's rubbing lotion onto his bare chest.

He caught me staring at him. "Figure out what?" he asked, his back against the locker.

I wanted to tell him to please put some clothes on.

"Why do some of the stories on you keep referring to some anonymous source? I'm sure the league knows about your habits, so what's there to hide?"

"It's the things they don't know that have created the problem," he said, returning to sit on the bench across from me.

"And what exactly are those?"

"Sasha, only those in my close circle know the severity of it."

"Who's included in that circle? Other players?"

He latched his watch around his wrist.

"Sometimes. But it's also some really shady rich cats who have money to burn and just want to be at the tables with us."

"And they're not trustworthy?"

"Hell, no. You can't trust anybody who can afford to win or lose up to a hundred grand a night."

"That's a high price to pay for excitement."

"Something has to excite me. Basketball sure doesn't do it anymore."

I couldn't believe he'd said that. Maybe he had changed. The Phoenix I knew loved basketball and had once told me he'd play for free. He must've sensed my disappointment.

He slipped his wife beater over his head and casually said, "What if I told you I bet Mitchell five grand that I could get you back?"

"You bastard. I'm not working for you," I said, half pissed, but not surprised.

"I doubt that by the size of that contract I signed. You must be charging me for more than PR."

"You really are full of yourself."

"Sasha, seriously, I need to ask you something. You still have those FedEx packages, right?"

"What did you think I'd do with them?"

"I'm going to eventually need to get them," he said, turning his head away from me to put his earring on.

"Wait a minute. Phoenix, what's going on? Why are you acting so suspicious? I hope you haven't lost those diamonds in some stupid crap game."

"Do you know how I got those diamonds?" he asked, bending over to put on his socks.

"Not really," I lied. He'd never told me any of the details, but I'd overheard enough conversations to know that a jeweler he did business with had been killed en route from Chicago to New York. Soon after, Phoenix had given me the diamond-filled envelopes to store in my home safe.

"Forget about it."

He wasn't looking at me, so I knew there was more to it.

I stood up to punctuate what I had to say. "Forget, my ass. You haven't asked for those diamonds in all this damn time. Now all of a sudden when all this other shit is going on, you want them back. Gimme a break. What the hell is going on? 'Cause I refuse to get mixed up in your shit."

"You're not going to be mixed up in anything, all right?"

"Phoenix, if somebody wants them, then just give them back."

"I wasn't the one that took the shit. I just wound up with them after the fact."

"No, I wound up with them."

"And what the fuck is that supposed to mean?"

I stood up to leave. "That means I'm not giving up anything until you tell me what's going on."

"You said you didn't want to be involved."

"I'm already involved, so don't give me that shit."

"Calm down, okay."

"No, I'm not calming down. I should've known there was more to it than some damn gambling rumors. And you're right, you can't trust people who have nothing to lose."

He jumped up and yelled, "I got a whole fucking lot to lose, and I'm going to handle this on my own." His towel dropped to the floor, exposing his naked body.

"Forget the contract. I'm out of here, Phoenix."

"Fuck that. I'm paying your ass damn near a half-million dollars, and you're gonna take care of this shit." He gripped me with one arm so tightly, it was hard for me to breathe.

"But what about—" I sputtered.

"What about what?" he asked, his breath harsh against my face. Rather than kiss me, he held his lips close till I could feel his words on my tongue. "In all your figuring out, do you know what you're gonna do about this, about me and you?"

He pressed his hard body against mine. His dick lay like a weight against my thigh. What could I do? I was pinned between his arms and the locker. I wanted him to take me right there in that stinking-ass locker room. "I'm not doing this with you again," I managed to say into his mouth.

"Remember, you're the one who called me in the middle of the night."

"I . . . I called you because—"

"Because what? Because you wanted me."

This time he teased me with his tongue, running it over my lips until, no longer able to resist him, I drew him deep into my mouth. He popped the snap on my jeans, releasing the zipper at the same time.

"I don't . . ." I tried to say as he tugged at my low riding panties, making his way underneath their silkiness.

"Shut up, Sasha. You can't tell me that you don't want me."

A door slammed in the distance, and he backed off, snatched up his towel, and covered himself, giving me a chance to get away from him.

Downstairs in the limousine Trey waited for us and opened the door when he saw me coming. Sitting in the limo, I cursed myself for thinking I could work with Phoenix again. I swallowed hard, savoring the leftover taste of Phoenix inside my mouth.

Moments later Phoenix approached the car in another one of his tasteful designer suits, his white shirt collar open and his tie hanging loosely around his neck. He handed his bags to the driver, who stood holding the door open for him. He slid into the backseat, and I edged closer to my door.

I turned my head and looked out the window as if interested in the traffic. Trey, who sat across from us, asked Phoenix, "You still wanna do that thing?"

"You got it all set up, right?"

"It'll be eighty autographs, and you'll get eight grand cash."

"Good. You take the money and keep two for yourself."

"Bet."

Trey spoke into his cell phone, telling someone we'd be there in twenty minutes.

Phoenix turned to me. "We gotta make a stop." When I ignored him, he put his hand on my chin and turned my head toward his.

"I'm sorry about what happened in there. It's all business from here on out."

Without looking at him, I nodded my head, even though I wasn't sure if I believed him.

We wound up at the side entrance of the Millennium Hotel. I was glad he didn't ask me to go inside with them. I knew from the conversation that Phoenix was about to do one of his unofficial autograph signings. It wasn't a lot of money, but he did it to get what he referred to as "booty money."

He was a pro at it, so in less than an hour he and Trey were climbing back into the car. When we pulled up to the rear entrance of the Essex House, where he was staying, a delivery truck and an unoccupied team bus blocked the entrance.

Pulling around to the main doors, we were met by a swarm of reporters who barely waited for the limousine to come to a full stop. Phoenix looked at me.

I called inside to the hotel and told the front desk that Phoenix Carter was out front and to have security come out to assist. Within minutes hotel security was standing outside the car, along with a few officers from the NYPD. Trey, who over the years had become adept at handling the crowd, stood guarding the door, practically daring anybody to step forward.

The driver rolled down the inside window and I told him that I would be getting out first. I cracked the window and told Trey we were ready. The door opened, and the crowd closed in, anticipating Phoenix, but instead I stepped out, walked up to the closest microphone, and spoke.

"Mr. Carter is on his way to the Garden and does not have time to be interviewed. If you have any questions, I'll be glad to assist you." It was official; Phoenix was now my client, and the whole world knew it.

Phoenix climbed out, his eyes covered by sunglasses, no smiles and no comments. Trey led us through the path that hotel security had made. The media was relentless, and I could hear people asking for autographs.

I tried to listen to comments from the reporters to find out what possibly could have happened to cause this stir.

"Phoenix, is gambling messing up your chances for making it to the finals this year?"

"Is there any truth to the talk that you've been betting on NBA games?"

By the time we reached Phoenix's suite, his cell phone and mine were ringing. There was a knock at the door from a team assistant who'd come to tell Phoenix that the bus was departing early for the Garden because of all the media. Phoenix packed up the few things he had in the room.

"I can't help you if you don't tell me the truth."

Handing his bags over to the assistant he said, "We'll

meet at my office in Chicago 'cause I doubt if the team makes it to the next round of the playoffs. We'll be able to talk there. And Sasha, I really am sorry about what happened back there."

"Okay, but until then, Phoenix, remember you control your image, so don't go doing anything in private that you can't handle being on the front page of every newspaper across the country."

I was more than ready to return to Philly and had practically forgotten about meeting with Lyor when my cell phone rang.

"I see your client is on his way to the Garden. Does that mean you're ready for me now?"

"Where are you?" I asked, in need of a drink before heading home in Manhattan's rush-hour traffic.

"W Hotel, Times Square."

So I went from one man's hotel room to another. When I entered Lyor's suite, it was obvious from the spread he'd laid out that he'd had no doubt that I'd come. He was dressed in a pair of cream linen slacks and a matching button-down shirt that hung loosely outside his pants. I looked down to his feet, where he wore a pair of slip-on sandals.

"I am glad you could make it," he said, ushering me in the door.

"Me, too," I answered, exhausted after my encounter with Phoenix.

The television was turned to ESPN, and there I was on the screen, saving Phoenix from himself.

"I thought you said you *used* to be his assistant."

"I did, but he's now retained me to serve as his publicist."

"To cover up his gambling?"

"Isn't that what I'm always doing for people? Covering up something."

"Be careful, Sasha. Gambling can be a dirty habit. It should not be taken lightly, especially if a person gets in with the wrong crowd."

"I'd prefer not to discuss my clients right now, especially Phoenix Carter."

"Your wish is granted."

We sat at the table, and he placed a napkin on my lap, then poured me a glass of Lorina lemonade.

I watched him as he removed the lids from all the food he'd ordered. Grilled lobster tail, filet mignon, and roasted chicken breast.

"I didn't know what you'd like, so I ordered everything."

"I see, and everything looks scrumptious."

He began fixing my plate. "Since you don't want to discuss work, then I guess you don't want to hear about a project where I might be able to use your services."

"What project is that?" I asked, totally uninterested in work. My mind was still back in that locker room.

"The waterfront business that the governor wants to bring to Pennsylvania could use a person with your PR skills on their board."

If anything could take my mind off Phoenix, it was the piece of business I'd been salivating over. Maybe I'd take that ride with Lyor after all.

7

FAMILY

June

As Phoenix had projected, Chicago did not make it to the finals. With Memorial Day behind us, I took a few days off to prepare for the arrival of my son and his family.

Daddy claimed to be less than overjoyed about all the changes that were about to take place in his home. His grandson and family living there weren't going to change any of his habits. I assumed that meant he'd still bring his dates home. But I knew he wouldn't do anything to disrespect them. It seemed to me, though, that he'd been spending a lot of time with Clara, and I hoped that meant he was settling down.

My first task was to have Daddy's house cleaned. Clara had agreed to keep him out of the house for the day. I hired the cleaning service we used at the office to do a thorough spring cleaning. The dusting, vacuuming, and dirty windows were a little too much for me to handle on my own.

When Daddy and Clara came in that evening, he was surprised to find me waiting for them.

"Sasha, what the hell have you done? I could've cleaned my own house."

Clara paid him no attention. "But you didn't, Joe, so be quiet. Sasha, something smells good in here. You didn't tell me you'd be cooking."

"You were in on this too," he said, lifting the lid off the pot of Italian sausage and meatballs steeping in marinara sauce. "This is what I'm talking about. C'mon, Clara, fix me a plate." Daddy walked into the dining room and pulled his chair up to the table.

While Clara fixed Daddy's plate and sliced and buttered his bread, I sat at the table talking with him.

"Daddy, I'm worried about you. What's going on with the cancer? Is the medicine working?"

"I don't know, maybe you should ask my woman," he said, exchanging a smile with Clara.

"Daddy, I'm not joking."

"Sweetness, I think I'm gonna wind up having surgery. The medicine isn't shrinking it as fast as the doctor would like. I gotta go see Jerry and the oncologist next week. Now what's this I hear, you're working for Phoenix Carter again?"

"Before we get to that, you should know that I'm going to call Jerry tomorrow and find out for myself. Now, since you asked about Phoenix, I've already started to have second thoughts."

"Why, he ain't paying you right? That nigga got a

lotta money. Don't let him get over on you just because y'all got the hots for each other."

There was no need to be embarrassed now. "Then you *did* know something was going on between us."

"Damn straight. I'm your daddy. Now, how much is he paying you?"

"Almost half a million dollars, if I can put up with him for that long."

Daddy broke out laughing, "Sweetness, for a half-million dollars, you can put up with anything. Remember, you're a Borianni."

Clara chimed in. "Joe, money isn't everything."

"Thanks, Clara. But Daddy, there is somebody I might want you to meet."

"Who's that? You mean I might have another son-in-law after all these years?"

"He's a bank manager, and we're taking it slow, but I like him."

"That's good, 'cause when you get that money from Phoenix, you're gonna need to know what to do with it."

"Joe, all you think about is money," Clara added.

"Since we're on the subject of men, Trent's been calling me."

"Oh, my man Trent. Now, I really liked him."

"Daddy, you like them all. He wants to get together the next time he comes to town. But I don't know if it's a good idea. It ended pretty bad between us."

"The hell with all these niggas. You don't owe him nothing. Remember, like I always told you, you still my horse, even if you never win a race."

"I love you, Daddy."

"I love you, too, sweetness."

The next afternoon I waited anxiously at Philadelphia International Airport for Owen and his family. Owen had picked up a few pounds, and Deirdre had cut her hair to about two inches from her scalp. But it was my grandchildren, Lil O, who was now six, and his three-year-old sister, Jada, who brought me to tears.

"Ma, what's up? Look at you," Owen exclaimed, almost lifting me off the ground.

"Deirdre, what have you been feeding my son?"

"Hi, Sasha. It's not me. He needs to stop eating all them sweets."

"Ganny, Ganny, did you bring me something?" Lil O asked.

"Sure did. C'mon, let's get in the truck."

Upon seeing the Range, Owen wasted no time offering to drive. When he turned on the CD player and 50 Cent blared from the speakers, Owen laughed and asked, "Ma, what you been listening to?"

"Oh, just a little something my assistant picked out for me."

Owen had been fortunate to land a position as assistant vice principal at West Philadelphia High School. Deirdre, on the other hand, had applied to the local hospitals for a part-time nursing job but was more than happy to help out with Daddy once he'd had his surgery.

When we bulldozed our way through the front door, Daddy didn't know what to do with himself. Unbeknownst to me, he'd brought gifts for everybody and had enough cheese steaks and hoagies to feed a football team.

Owen was eating up everything and couldn't seem to stop talking about how glad he was to be home. If he weren't such a tough guy, I think he'd have been crying by now. When the children began to get cranky, I gave them a bath and read them *Goodnight Moon* until they both fell asleep.

It was past ten when I got home. I called Phoenix, who'd been on vacation.

"Sasha, I was going to call you. Did I miss anything?"

"Not really. There's still some stuff floating in the newspapers, but you haven't been on the front page of the sports section."

"Good. Good. Now, when are you coming to Chicago? I want to get this thing cleared up. My camp starts next week, and then I have a celebrity game in Memphis that I'm playing in."

"Fine, I'll make the travel arrangements."

After speaking with him, I was determined to track down Arshell, who seemed to be taking a vacation from our friendship.

Luckily, she was awake and more than willing to talk. I told her about Jordan, and she found it hard to believe that I had yet to sleep with him. I thought she'd be glad that I hadn't, but she kept saying, What if I was doing all this dating and then he turned out to be a dud? This was so unlike Arshell. She'd always been the one to tell me to take it slow and try to make a real relationship. Then I brought her up-to-date on Phoenix. She wasn't the least bit surprised that he was back, but she added, "You know he still has the power and money to lure you back into bed."

Boy, did that make me feel cheap. What the hell was going on with her and this sudden change?

"You've heard my news. Now, what's up with you?"

"All I can say is, get ready, because you won't be far behind."

"Far behind in what?"

"I'm going through what's called transitioning into menopause."

I guess I'd never really given menopause much thought. I just expected to look up one day and find my period gone. "What do you mean transitioning? Has your period stopped?"

"No, the transition means I've started having all the damn symptoms, you know, like heavy periods one month and none the next. My hair is all broken off, and sometimes in the middle of the night I have to wake up and change the bed linens because I've perspired so much."

"Arshell, I had no idea. Is there anything you can take?"

"What for? It's Mother Nature. I've tried some stuff, but nothing really works." I was sure she had, since by occupation she was a pharmacist. "No matter what you take, Sasha, it doesn't stop you from feeling all used up as a woman."

I was taken aback by her statement. Arshell had always been the one to make me believe that I was worth more than I thought myself to be. I didn't want to be selfish, but I couldn't handle it if she started falling apart.

"The kids really don't need me anymore—the twins are in the seventh grade, and Lisa will be starting college next year."

"Arshell, why didn't you tell me this sooner? I'm so sorry. I've been busy, with Owen moving back and Daddy and the firm."

"Stop it, girl. It's not that bad. I do get some relief."

"I'm confused. So you *are* taking something?"

She laughed before answering. "Yeah, I guess you could say that."

"What are you talking about?" My instincts told me I wasn't going to like the answer.

"I can't talk about it right now. Wayne just came in. I'll probably come up to see you in a few weeks, okay?"

"No, it's not okay. I wanna know what you're doing."

"Chill out. I'll tell you everything when I see you."

On Saturday night Jordan called and told me to be dressed for church on Sunday morning. That was something I hadn't done in a long time, except when I'd visited Pastor Price's church, but that was business. As a child I hadn't been much of a churchgoer, even though Daddy had insisted that I attend Sunday school until I was twelve.

Being asked to accompany Jordan to church, though, was a clear indication that he intended to make me his Sunday showpiece. I didn't have a problem with that. To look the part, I chose a lined white linen suit—cropped jacket with two buttons, and a skirt that hit me just above the knees. I finished my ensemble with a colorful Hermès blouse.

Jordan arrived Sunday morning at ten o'clock sharp in a navy blue, single-breasted, three-button suit, with a red-and-blue polka-dot bow tie.

"Don't you look good this morning?" I said before kissing him.

"And you, too. Are you ready?"

"Yep," I answered, grabbing my purse off the couch.

Driving up Roosevelt Boulevard to Greater Zion Baptist

Church, we found ourselves in the uncomfortable position of discussing the pros and cons of being in a relationship.

"Sasha, tell me, when's the last time you've been in a real relationship?"

I'm not sure what, if anything, I wanted to share with him about my past lovers. "It's been a while, probably about two, maybe three years." I was speaking about Trent, of course.

"What happened?"

"It just wasn't working out. We had two different ideas of where we were going." I'm not sure where that answer came from, so I posed the same question to him.

"Well, honestly . . . ," he started. I hated when people start an answer with honestly—it meant they were going to lie. "I thought I was in love. Just about a year ago, the woman I was in love with didn't think I was ready to settle down, so I walked away from the relationship."

He was definitely lying. This was good. We were on our way to church and lying about our past relationships.

"And are you still in love with her?" I hoped he wasn't but was almost positive he was, or we wouldn't be having this conversation.

"No. I guess I just felt getting married was the proper thing to do, in addition to the right career move."

I wondered if I could ever really be a wife again. It was so long ago that I'd been married to Owen's father. Sometimes I forgot I'd ever been married. "Why all the questions, Jordan?"

"Sooner or later we're bound to sleep together, at least I'm hoping so, if we can ever stop working," he said, his eyes on me instead of on the road. "I need to know if you still have a flame or two for one of your old boyfriends."

"No flames for me," I lied, thinking of my run-ins with Phoenix and Trent.

"Me neither," he lied, adjusting the rearview mirror when he'd already been driving for twenty minutes.

I was relieved when we pulled up in front of the church, cutting short our conversation.

Standing in the narthex, I took in the building's beautiful woodwork, stained-glass windows, and cathedral ceiling. Jordan held my hand as the usher escorted us to a pew about five rows from the front. Every pew in the church was full, even though the bulletin read that there had been an earlier service. Reading the church bulletin, I discovered Jordan's name was listed as chairman of the New Building Fund.

After the opening prayer and readings from the Bible the choir began a rendition of "Jesus, You're the Center of My Joy" that sounded more like an R&B tune. The minister, whose pulpit sat up so high we had to look up at him, preached about making a conscious decision to renew your relationship with God.

After the service, Jordan spoke or nodded to everyone, and introduced me to a lot of people. It was amusing that my presence there drew so much attention. Whatever game Jordan was playing or whomever he was trying to make jealous, I'm sure it worked. I'd noticed there was one particular woman who during the service kept stealing glances at me from under her wide-brim hat. Jordan, however, failed to introduce us.

8

CROSSING THE LINE

August

Owen and Deirdre, who had yet to see my new office, dropped by unexpectedly one morning. I was in a client meeting when they arrived. Kendra volunteered to show them around the suite, and I caught up with them in my office when I finished.

Deirdre was impressed with how I'd been able to work my way out of my home office, becoming, according to *Good Day Philadelphia,* the head of Philadelphia's premier African-American public relations firm. I would've preferred to drop the African-American label, but that was a battle I was still fighting. Owen, too, was pleased, but I could see he was more interested in Tiffany, whom he kept stealing glances at.

I looked at Owen as only a mother could and said, "She is off limits."

"Ma, I wouldn't do that."

"Owen, there is something I want to talk to you about."

"What? Grandpa's surgery?"

"No, it's about me. I've contracted to do some work for Phoenix Carter."

"Ma, I think it's a bad idea. I hope you haven't forgotten what happened with you and him last time."

"How can I forget? Shit, everybody keeps reminding me."

"What about this guy Jordan? He seems pretty nice."

"Believe me, Jordan is, but one thing has nothing to do with the other."

"Maybe you're right, but Phoenix is more rich and powerful than he was before."

"Trust me, son, that's my point. Phoenix's account could mean a lot of money and global publicity for Platinum Images."

"Enough for me to get a little Denali or something?"

"Oh, so if you get something out of it, then it's okay? To hell with your mother."

"No, Ma, I'm only joking. I just don't wanna have to hurt that nigga. I don't care who he is."

"Not to worry. Nobody's gonna get hurt." But as soon as I'd said it, I didn't believe it.

The best part of the day was that I was having lunch with Lyor. He was picking me up at noon for what he said would be an unforgettable date. The receptionist buzzed me around twelve-fifteen saying that Mr. Turrell was waiting curbside. I couldn't understand why Lyor hadn't come upstairs but figured he'd probably had trouble finding a parking space, so I grabbed my purse and headed to the lobby.

Walking past Kendra's desk, I found her wrapped up in the phone cord, haggling with a vendor. When I stopped at her desk to tell her I was going to lunch, she put her hand over the mouthpiece and said, "You know, my grandmother always said it's not respectable for a man to meet you outside."

"I'll remember that next time."

When I stepped outside, I looked for what I assumed he'd be driving, a Jaguar or maybe even a two-seater Benz. But I stopped short when I saw Lyor leaning against what looked like a new, or at least very clean, black and sterling silver Harley-Davidson motorcycle.

If he thought I was riding on the back of that thing, he was out of his mind. "Am I following you?" I asked, one hand on my hip, staring at what really was a gorgeous piece of machinery.

Blowing a bubble from the big wad of gum he was chewing, he let it pop before responding, "I was hoping you were riding with me."

"You gotta be kidding. First, I don't do motorcycles, and second, I don't think I should do it in a dress."

He switched his helmet from one hand to the other. "The first one you have to decide, but I will tell you that I ride safely and would never endanger you or myself. I have already solved the question of what you will wear," he said, handing me a rather large leather duffel bag that had been strapped to his seat.

Lyor and I had spoken several times since I'd seen him in New York, but now outside in the daylight, I took him in. His long narrow face held a sharp beaklike nose that was underlined by thin lips. His closely cut hair fell in small dark brown curls. But even with his white-boy looks and his model body, he came off rather rough around the edges dressed in worn jeans, a T-shirt, and black Timberland boots.

"Well, since you came bearing gifts, that could change any girl's mind." I answered, taking the bag from his leather-gloved hand.

Back in my office, I unzipped the bag, anxious to see its contents. Inside I found a faded pair of D&G jeans that I knew were every bit of $700, and a white T-shirt with D&G embroidered on the front. Still digging I came up with a yellow Harley-Davidson windbreaker and a pair of Adidas sneakers, all in my size.

I changed clothes, checked myself out in the mirror, and, liking what he'd purchased, headed back outside. Halfway down the steps, Tiffany caught up with me.

"Who's the new beau?" she asked from the landing outside her office.

"I'm not sure yet if he's a beau or a client."

"I didn't know you liked white boys."

"You seem to forget I'm half white." I'd never really said that before in defense of anything, but somehow I felt I needed to defend my date with Lyor, even though I had no idea what it would amount to.

"Whatever you say."

Back outside, I was ready to mount Lyor's bike. I threw one leg over the side. He helped to position my butt on the long leather seat. Placing his hands on my hips, he asked if I was comfortable.

"Now, listen. This is how we are going to do this. You

have to hold on tight to me around the waist." He didn't have to worry about that.

"While we are riding, just move your body with mine as if we were, well, dancing, okay?" I nodded my head yes, along with the big helmet that he'd strapped under my chin.

Nestling his body into the space in front of me, he stepped down on the pedal and revved the engine.

We began our descent down Main Street and onto Ridge Avenue. I wasn't so afraid on the city streets, but once he started up the ramp toward the Schuylkill Expressway, my belly flipped and my grip around his waist got tighter. I felt totally unprotected against the cars and trucks that whizzed by us.

By the time we passed the Spring Garden Street exit, he'd settled into a steady speed. My body moved with his, bending with the curves in the road. My fear eased up, and even though I was afraid, I found his way of traveling exciting.

Exiting at South Street, he made a right and headed over Thirty-first Street toward Chestnut. I was sure he didn't own part of Drexel University, but he continued until he brought the bike to a stop in front of a blue awning displaying a sign that read "Left Bank Apartments."

Lyor climbed off the bike, removed his helmet, and helped me off by holding onto my hips to steady my wobbly legs.

"As promised, we have arrived safely," he said.

"You were really good out there," I replied, stretching my legs out.

"I've been doing this for a while."

The doorman stepped outside and nodded to Lyor.

Looking in my direction, he said, "Welcome to the Smart Side of the City!"

I wasn't sure how I was supposed to respond, so I smiled and wondered to myself if that meant that the neighborhood north of Market Street, where people I knew lived, was considered dumb.

Inside the Left Bank's small lobby, Lyor turned into a businessman as he began telling me about the renovation of the old Pennsylvania Railroad building. I could only hope that he wasn't as anal as Jordan.

"This is one of the first Philadelphia properties I had the privilege of investing in. It is also one of Philadelphia's largest historical properties. I've converted it to private residences."

I followed him as he pointed out two conference rooms and a cozy library. A private parking garage in the rear of the building led to a convenient on-site Italian restaurant.

Exiting the elevator on the fourth floor, we walked down a long hallway that was clearly a part of the original architecture. He used his passkey to unlock one of the unoccupied units.

"How much does a renovation like this cost?" I asked, looking around at the stark white apartment.

"Roughly $58 million," he answered. "I lived here for a few months near the end of the renovation and moved out just recently."

"And where do you live now?"

I imagined he would say the Art Museum area or even Old City, but was surprised when he answered, "Camden."

We walked through the apartment in silence, just admiring the dramatic round columns, wood moldings, and large windows, all of which he said were part of the original structure.

"Lyor, I want to apologize for being so distracted during dinner in New York. That was really nice of you not only to arrange dinner but to offer me a seat on the board of the waterfront project."

"No need to apologize, but know that if you ever need to talk about business, I'm available."

"Thanks, I'll keep that in mind."

"Now, as I was about to say, you may already know this, but the building in which Platinum Images is housed used to be an old textile mill."

"Is that the reason why my lease is so expensive?"

"That and the fact that you're in Manayunk. You should consider purchasing it; you could make a lot of money when you sell it."

"That's something to consider. See, you're giving me business advice already."

"I'm sure I could help you a lot more."

Not knowing what he really meant, I didn't answer. Instead I walked over to open the sliding glass doors. As he stood behind me, his breath tickled the back of my neck. "The Left Bank is the only complex in the city that has an interior atrium courtyard."

I watched the landscapers hard at work preparing the grounds. The ruins from the old building stood in the middle of the narrow courtyard and reminded me of an artifact from Greece.

But my mind pondered what type of person this Lyor Turrell was, and why he was interested in me, excluding the obvious reason.

"Would you like to eat before we go to our next destination?" he asked, taking me out of my thoughts and leading me by the hand toward the door.

"That's right. You did promise me lunch."

Our next stop was Rittenhouse Square's Devon Seafood Grille, where we sat curbside and ordered lunch. I learned that Lyor was born in Tel Aviv, Israel, but came to the United States when he was ten years old. He was a graduate of Hofstra University in New York and held degrees in global marketing and finance. He'd taken a chance while in grad school on a piece of high-end real estate, and now he had a keen eye for turning real estate deals into cash cows.

"What about your siblings? Are they also involved in the family business?"

"My sister is a jeweler in New York, another business we've had in the family for over a hundred years, and my brother is a rabbi." A faraway look came into his eyes. He continued, "And my oldest brother died a few years ago."

"I'm sorry to hear that." The last thing I wanted to talk about was death. I changed the subject and said, "The jewelry business must be interesting. I've never understood the world's obsession with diamonds."

"Does that mean diamonds aren't your best friend? I mean, judging from what I saw you wear, you might have a slight obsession," he said, referring to the diamonds he'd seen me wearing the night of my open house.

"Most of them were gifts—but I mean, people are so infatuated with diamonds. Especially this whole hip-hop generation."

"One day I'll tell you all about that business. But the business I want to discuss with you now is the upcoming waterfront project."

"What's the status of that, anyway? I know you said

the governor was in support of it. Any movement with the city yet?"

"I don't get Philadelphia. They complain that they're buried in debt, yet when we propose a surefire way to bring money into the city and to help their dying school system, they back off. But I have confidence that it will happen."

"I guess I waver on that line too."

"How so?"

"I mean, it's definitely going to cause people to gamble irresponsibly, which will probably cause a rise in crime, so it's a no-win situation."

"Sasha, there's always going to be crime but there will also be jobs, and your mayor will be able to get Philadelphia out of the red. Now, I hope your wavering won't keep you from sitting on the board, because my thought is, since you handle so much PR for Philadelphia, you could make sure that the ratio for minorities is filled in all aspects of the project."

I was insulted. "Is that all you think I can handle, ensuring minority workers and businesses are treated fairly? Why can't Platinum Images be the lead public relations firm on the project? Or is that saved for the good ol' white PR firms?"

"Obviously I've gotten a rise out of you. I like it."

"I just hate being pigeonholed into one type of business."

"No, no, I like it. I cannot wait to see what else gets a rise out of you."

I laughed at him and to chill myself out. "What does Lyor Turrell do when he's not making deals?"

"That is a rare occurrence. But I will tell you, if you promise to go with me, that I just love going down to

Naples, Florida, and passing time at the greyhound dog races."

"That's it? No baseball, no hockey?"

"Are you now pigeonholing me? I do like those sports, but betting on the dogs is fun, you'd like it. It's a big sport down there."

Thinking of Phoenix, I said, "You're a bit of a gambler yourself, uh?"

"Only for fun. Certainly not like your client."

After lunch Lyor and I headed over the Ben Franklin Bridge toward New Jersey. Obviously he'd saved the best for last. The Victor, which was located on Camden, New Jersey's waterfront, was a property I'd read about in the *New York Times,* but I wasn't aware that it had opened yet.

The Victor was the old RCA Building, where they'd done a $60 million renovation. The entrance tower included a symbol of Nipper the Dog staring into a twentieth-century Victrola. When I read about the Victor, I'd been curious about what it would look like when it was finished, and I thought that maybe one day I'd give up my house in Chestnut Hill and move to a nice maintenance-free condo. I was looking forward to seeing it firsthand.

After dismounting the bike, Lyor pulled it up on the sidewalk, where the doorman greeted us and told Lyor that he'd keep an eye on it. Judging by the number of contractors around the building, it was obvious that it wasn't finished. I just hoped it was safe. According to Lyor, the building wouldn't be finished until September. He had an apartment inside, where he was living until the renovations were completed. I wondered if he had a permanent home anywhere.

Before going up to his condo, we went inside to the rental office so he could pick up some packages. He introduced me to one of the leasing agents, who, though pleasant, gave me the once-over. Lyor must've noticed it too, because he placed his hand in mine as we walked out the door.

Even with everything I'd read about the Victor, Lyor's fifth-floor condo was so much more than I expected. Walking into his apartment, I was amazed at all the detailing and the historical architecture. The apartment was thirteen hundred square feet of space, with two bedrooms and two baths.

While checking his voice mail, Lyor rummaged through mail that was on top of his kitchen counter. While he opened his packages, he told me, "Look around, tell me how you like this place."

As he returned phone calls I took in the condo's breathtaking view of the Ben Franklin Bridge, the Philly skyline, and the Delaware River. I could only imagine what it looked like at night.

I caught snippets of his phone conversation. I didn't want to eavesdrop, but it was hard not to, so I roamed through the apartment, which was unfurnished except for one beautiful leather-and-fabric chair that sat next to the window with a matching footstool. Facing it was a flat-screen television that had been mounted on the wall.

"Tell him that's my last offer. What do you mean, you can't talk to him like that? I don't give a damn who he is. Let me be clear, I will not allow anybody to dictate my business. Can you make him understand that, or do I have to handle it myself?"

Damn, he was letting somebody have it. Maybe I didn't want to do business with him.

"My apologies for handling business, but some things

cannot be helped," he said as he hung up the phone. "Tell me, do you like the Victor?"

"How often do you stay here?"

"Not much. But now that I have met you, I hope to have a reason to stay home."

"You sound pretty sure of yourself."

"I shouldn't?" When I didn't answer, he continued, "Why don't we have a drink? I think I can find something you like." He headed to the kitchen, where he pulled a bottle of Hennessy Paradis out of the cabinet.

My cell phone and Blackberry buzzed simultaneously. The call was from Kendra, reminding me that I had a six o'clock dinner meeting at Alma De Cuba. She was also sending my messages through the Blackberry in case I wasn't back to the office before she left for the day.

When I finished my call, Lyor stood waiting with the glasses and bottle on the windowsill.

"Shall we share in a toast?"

"What would the occasion be?"

"I guess I should say business, but I am hoping for so much more."

We raised our glasses and toasted. "To our budding relationship," he said. "C'mon, let's sit." He motioned for me to sit in the room's only chair, while he sat on the footstool facing me.

Sinking into the chair's soft leather, I said, "Now, that's comfortable."

"Tell me all about Sasha Borianni."

"I have a son, Owen, who's twenty-six years old. He and his wife Deirdre and my two beautiful grandchildren, Lil Owen and Jada, just recently moved to Philadelphia from Los Angeles."

"Where are they living?"

"With my father, who will probably have to undergo surgery for prostate cancer."

"Is he going to be okay?"

"Yes, the doctors say he should be just fine."

"You seem to have a lot going on, and you haven't even mentioned business."

"Business is great. It demands most of my time. I'd be bored to death without it."

"What is the excitement in controlling someone's image?

"Key word would be *control,* especially when PR is so unpredictable."

"And what about your personal life?"

"I guess I really haven't made the time for a personal life," I said, disregarding the time I'd been enjoying with Jordan. "Enough about me. Why haven't *you* been snagged?"

"Pure selfishness. I have no interest in living the same routine day after day."

"And how do you define excitement?"

My cell phone went off again. This time it was Deirdre, asking me if I was still picking up the kids on Saturday. After speaking with her, I returned to the conversation.

He rested his hand on my thigh and leaned into me. "One thing is certain. Sasha Borianni has already begun to excite me. It's only my hope I can do the same for her."

9

SPIN CONTROL

Daddy had scheduled his surgery, and I often found myself wondering if I would lose him. It was a thought that often would bring on a panic attack. After having Jordan unknowingly talk me through one of my personal trips over the phone, I was awakened at almost midnight by the ringing of the phone.

"Sasha, I'm sorry to call you so late, but I'm on my way to Philly and was hoping we could have breakfast in the morning."

"Trent?"

"Yeah, baby. It's me. You want to have breakfast?"

"I guess. Where are you staying? The Marriott?"

"No, I'm going to be at the Four Seasons. Can you be there by eight o'clock?"

"Yes."

"Perfect."

Falling back to sleep wasn't easy, since having breakfast with him had to fit into an already packed day. Owen was taking me to the airport in the afternoon because I was meeting with Phoenix in Chicago, and I still had to finish packing.

After a fitful night's sleep, punctuated by dreams of Daddy's funeral and Phoenix being suspended from the league, I woke up panicked that I was late for breakfast with Trent. I didn't want to take a Paxil, for fear that I wouldn't be fully alert for what Trent had to say, if anything.

I went from one closet to another, trying to figure out what to wear. Sexy, professional, casual, sluttish—whatever I wore would send a message, and it had to be the right one. I pulled out a pair of vintage Levi's and a midnight blue sleeveless wrap shirt. That would have to do.

By the time I stepped into the shower, I was a nervous wreck. I stood under the showerhead and let the hot water beat on my body for as long and hard as I could stand it. I began lathering myself with my favorite perfumed shower gel. It felt good having my soapy hands caress my skin, and before I realized it, I'd gone too far. With one hand I held onto the bar as the other slipped between my thighs and lingered on my clit. I allowed myself to imagine the feel of Trent's beard against my thighs, the tip of his tongue running the length of me. I could've stayed like that all day, but the water went shockingly cold and I had to quickly rinse off and jump out.

Walking into the Fountain restaurant at the Four Seasons, I spotted Trent right away. I'd expected him to be dressed in a suit, but he wore jeans and a striped polo shirt. I was glad I'd dressed casually, too.

He kissed me on the cheek and pulled out my chair. "Good morning, Sasha. I'm so glad you could make it on such short notice."

Now I wasn't sure if this was business or pleasure. I mean, what category did wanting-to-catch-up fall under? "Good morning, Trent. You don't look dressed for a meeting."

"It doesn't start until noon. It's a luncheon."

"I'm not quite clear on how New Jersey politics brings you to Philadelphia so often."

"Why don't you be honest and say you're confused about why I wanted to see you?"

"Are you saying I have a problem being honest?"

"Sasha, look, I don't want to argue with you. That's definitely not why I wanted to see you."

"Then why, Trent? Why am I here?"

Before answering, he ordered breakfast for the two of us, remembering that I liked my eggs scrambled soft.

"What if I told you I've missed you?"

"Trent, I can't believe you asked me to breakfast to tell me you missed me. I thought you wanted to catch up, so that's what we will do. I have my own business now, Platinum Images, as you know. Daddy is about to undergo surgery for prostate cancer. Owen, Deirdre, and my grandkids live here now. I have a man in my life, and I'm working for Phoenix Carter again. Now it's your turn." He had to back off now.

"My daughter Briana is a junior at NYT; my son TJ is four, and I see him every other weekend. I too have a friend in my life. Her name is Veronica, and she's a buyer at Barney's. The reason why I'm in Philadelphia so often is because I'm working on the committee to stop waterfront gambling from ruining Philadelphia."

Our food arrived, and with all that said, I didn't know what to do next. Out of nowhere Trent just started laughing, and before I knew it I was laughing, too.

"Look, Sasha, I know we both kept secrets from each other, and I'm probably wrong for even being here with you, but if nothing else, I want us to be friends. I plan to be in Philadelphia a lot. From time to time I'd really like to see you. I mean, if that's all I can get."

Looking at him, I told myself how I would've liked to have given him so much more.

"Trent, I would like that, too."

We sat talking for over an hour about our lives and the waterfront project, especially when I told him I was on the committee in favor of the project. By the end of our breakfast, I think we both knew that it would be best for us to stay friends.

By ten-thirty I was back home and waiting for Owen to pick me up. He was anxious to take me to the airport because I was letting him hold the Range Rover, in exchange for him doing some small repairs on the house.

"How's your job coming along now that school has started?"

"It's different from what I expected."

"What do you mean?"

"Things have changed in Philly since I went to school here. Some of the teachers dress worse than the students. I just don't think they should be able to wear jeans and stuff, so I've chosen to be an example and wear a suit every day."

"My son, the rebel. That's your biggest challenge, the dress code. What about teaching?"

"There won't be much of that going on for me. Ma,

there are so many teenagers in high school on probation wearing ankle bracelets that it's almost like a small prison. When you mix that in with the girls who are pregnant, it's overwhelming. I don't even know where to start."

"Son, do like your mother and jump right smack in the middle."

Comfortably seated in first class, I settled in for the direct flight to Chicago. I loved Chicago and had always wanted to return, but after my run with Phoenix, I'd lost interest in the city and anything that reminded me of him.

I'd agreed to stay overnight and have dinner with Phoenix, so he was putting me up at the Hotel Monaco, which was located in the heart of downtown.

Trey picked me up from O'Hare in a black-on-black 2004 Excursion with heavily tinted windows. He waited outside my hotel while I showered and changed into a thin navy pin-striped skirt suit, a silk tank underneath with a contrasting polka-dot Kate Spade scarf. I put dabs of my Marc Jacobs perfume around my ankle and at the top of my thighs.

Once Trey dropped me off in front of the high-rise smoked-glass building that housed Carter Enterprises, I was met in the lobby by one of Phoenix's many assistants and whisked into his private elevator, taking me to his penthouse office on the forty-second floor.

After seating me in the conference room, the young lady told me she would let Mr. Carter know that I'd arrived. The conference room was humongous, with a large rectangular table and chairs for what looked like over twenty-five people. The floor-to-ceiling windows that covered one wall made the room seem even larger, if not a little scary, as I stood looking out at all of Chicago.

I poured myself a glass of fresh-squeezed orange juice from the assortment of drinks on the buffet and took a seat; the feeling of being suspended in air was making me dizzy, and that was last thing I wanted to be.

If I had not been sitting when Phoenix walked in, I might have had to, as he was wearing the most beautifully tailored suit that had ever graced a man's body.

"Damn, what'd you do? Just have that suit made this morning?"

"Oh, does this work?" he exclaimed, running his hands over the lapels, exposing his shirtsleeve, which held an exquisite pair of diamond and gold cufflinks. He walked over to me and kissed me on the forehead. "Was your trip in okay?"

"Yes, it was fine."

"C'mon, let me show you around." He took me back into the hall, where he introduced me to his modestly attractive executive assistant. We continued through an open doorway, directly into his office—if that is what one would call it.

His spacious office was richly furnished. A formidable mahogany desk, a conference table, and a seven-foot L-shaped couch faced four twenty-five-inch television screens that lined the wall. Large prints by E. N. Brown and a charcoal replica of Phoenix on the court lined the adjacent wall. On his credenza there was a picture of his children, and a separate frame held a picture of his wife Crystal.

"Phoenix, you really have grown up."

"You like it? I had to have all this shit custom-made to fit my long ass."

The sultry voice of Vivian Green flowed from a set of unseen speakers. Checking out the two walls of windows, I asked, "Don't you get dizzy being in here?"

"Shit, I'm never here." He seated himself behind the desk. Rocking back and forth in his leather swivel chair, he looked like a big kid. "Do you think this gambling shit is going to kick back up again when the season starts?"

"As sure as my name is Sasha Borianni."

"Damn, I been trying to be cool, but this shit is tough. What's your plan? I know you got something for me."

"It's in my briefcase."

"Sasha, c'mon now. I know you still don't have that Gucci one, do you?" he asked, rising from his chair.

"It's in perfect shape," I said, remembering that was one of the first gifts he'd given me. "Ready to get started?"

"I haven't finished showing you my office yet," he said, walking toward a door to his left. I followed him through the door, which opened into a smaller office, where it actually looked as if someone worked. Now this was the Phoenix Carter I knew. There were two basketballs in the corner, an overstuffed couch where he probably slept sometimes, and a thirty-two-inch television that was turned to SportsCenter.

"I'd be correct to assume that this office," I said, pointing to the larger office, "is for show and—"

"You're right. This one is for working."

At that point his assistant buzzed him and said they were ready to start. When we returned to the conference room, Mitchell, two other lawyers, Phoenix's in-house PR person, and his assistant were already there.

Once Phoenix introduced me to everyone, I started the meeting by distributing a two-page brief. "Up until now Phoenix has had a carefully honed image that made him the NBA's most marketable athlete; however, at the end of the season an anonymous source began threatening that image with unfounded rumors."

Mitchell piped in, "I should tell you now that on my way here I received a call from the editor at the *Chicago Tribune,* who says his source has agreed to come forward."

"What? When the fuck were you gonna tell me? That's bullshit! Who the hell is the damn source, Mitchell?"

"He won't tell me unless you agree to do an exclusive."

"That'll never happen," I mumbled.

"Everybody has a fucking angle."

Mitchell continued his assessment. "Sounds to me like somebody is carefully strategizing. They started these rumors in February right after All Star break, and then all summer it gets quiet, and now that you're about to go to training camp, the rumor mill starts back up again."

"What's the NBA head office saying?" I asked.

"They've called a meeting in two weeks."

"Mitchell, you'll be with him?"

"Certainly. He is *my* client."

"Can you make sure you ask them for the go-ahead to hold a press conference?"

"I won't let the NBA fuck with me on this. They'd better have my damn back."

"Phoenix, they'd be cutting their own throats if they acted too soon. You can be certain that the league recognizes that your presence has generated more money than any athlete in their history," I said to reassure him of where he stood.

"What about my reputation with the fans?"

"The rumors won't change a thing. Just to be certain, I have a company in Philly that can track changes in your popularity," I replied.

"Sasha, how do you plan to put a spin on this?" Mitchell asked.

"What we're going to do is play a little image roulette. I mean, until these allegations are proven, Phoenix still runs Chicago and the league."

Mitchell snorted. "I'm sure you can spin this shit until the media is dizzy."

I turned my gaze to Mitchell. I'd had about enough of him. I knew he didn't like having me back on board. He was well aware that Phoenix would likely do whatever I suggested.

"Fuck that, Mitchell. You act like the shit is true. I'll retire before I go under, and believe me, I won't go under alone," Phoenix responded sharply.

"The plan I came here with has to be changed to Plan B, that's all. And that'll also depend on what happens at your meeting with the commissioner. We will do damage control if things begin to leak again, but let's not forget all the positive press you received over the summer."

"Yes, you had him give away a lot of money. To charity."

Mitchell was more concerned about how much money Phoenix would lose if his career was ruined than he was with his reputation.

"And while you're putting a spin on my reputation, what are we supposed to do about making sure my endorsers don't pull out?"

"No one has pulled out of anything because they don't have a reason. And, Mitchell, isn't that what you get paid for? To make sure they don't."

"I'm well aware of my job."

None of the other meeting participants said anything; at this point there was no need to. Phoenix was clearly pissed that Mitchell had waited until this meeting to tell him about the *Chicago Tribune.* When he saw that Mitchell and I were about to go at it, he told everyone they were dismissed. That is, except me.

Phoenix went over to the window and looked back at me. When he didn't say anything, I asked, "What's wrong?"

"Nothing's wrong. I'm just glad to have you back."

"Better not let Mitchell hear you say that."

"Fuck him. You ready to get something to eat so we can talk?"

"Sure."

"Let me change. I'll be right back."

When we stepped outside, I expected to see the Excursion I'd arrived in, but slowly rolling from around the corner was a chauffeur-driven two-toned black Mercedes Benz, the likes of which I'd never seen before. Obviously, I'd forgotten how it was to travel with Phoenix Carter.

Laughing at my reaction, Phoenix said, "It's a Maybach. You're gonna love it. Get in."

The driver stood holding the door for us.

"I've never seen anything like it," I commented, as I stepped into what had to be the highest-quality automobile I'd ever seen.

"You won't, either, because so far they've only made about five hundred of them."

"And I thought my Range Rover was luxury."

"You finally got rid of that ol'-ass Accord."

I gave him a quick glare to remind him that he'd taken back the BMW and Lexus truck he'd given me when our relationship fell apart. But there was no need to go back down that road.

Like a little kid, he pointed out the four-zone climate control for each seat, in addition to the fact that the seats reclined and his legs actually fit comfortably. He turned up the volume on the Dolby surround system that was linked to twin flat-screen monitors.

"You're so damn rich, it's disgusting."

"Believe it or not, I helped design it to fit me personally. Here," he said, flipping down the compartment where his wireless laptop with Internet access was stored.

"Is there anything left for you to buy?"

"Besides out of the bullshit I'm in now, not really."

As we set out, I noticed that Trey followed us in the Excursion. Our first stop was my hotel, where I changed into a pair of Burberry jeans and a blouse. Before leaving the room, I noticed a familiar brown box tied with gold ribbon. There was no doubting that Phoenix had had it delivered to my room while we were in the meeting. Untying the ribbon and removing the dustcover, I found a beautiful Louis Vuitton Sorbonne briefcase made with Epi leather. Hell, maybe I did need a new briefcase, after all.

Getting back in the car, I could tell by his tone that he was on the phone with his wife Crystal. When he finished I asked how she and the children were handling the scandal.

"Not too damn well," he said. "They're up in the Hamptons with her sister right now, and that's where they need to stay."

"Phoenix, thanks for the bag."

"Forget that shit. What you wanna eat?"

Rather than go somewhere where the media would be expecting him, we went to Chicago's South Side and wound up at Lem's BBQ. We stayed seated in the car while Trey went inside to survey the crowd. Once he told us it was cool, Phoenix walked in and nodded to people but didn't allow his eyes to linger a minute too long; people would take it as invitation to come over and say hello.

Trey and the other two security people sat at a table close by. Trey had worked for Phoenix since he'd joined the league, and I wondered if there was anything he didn't know about Phoenix. In a rear booth over beer, ribs, and chicken, Phoenix and I caught up with each other's personal lives. He also wanted to know about my sex life, as all ex-lovers do when they know that they've served you well.

"There is a brother, a bank manager."

"You with a banker? Sounds kind of boring."

"Very funny, but actually he's not."

"What happened with Trent?"

I knew this would come up eventually.

"Just didn't work out."

"If I was a part of the reason you two never got married, I really am sorry. My ass has been sorry about a lot of things lately where you're concerned. I guess I'm just trying to be a mature, professional athlete, that's all."

We both laughed at that joke.

After dinner we rode in the Maybach along Lakeshore Drive. By now we'd talked about everything except his gambling. I didn't want to waste any more time, and I knew if given the chance Phoenix would slip away in the night with us never having talked.

"How bad is the gambling?" I asked, unsure if he'd heard me.

"You sure you wanna know?" The way he said it made

me think that maybe I didn't want to know, but it was too late for that now. He picked up the car's intercom phone and told the driver to pull over. Trey pulled up alongside us in the Excursion, and we switched cars.

I had no idea why my question called for the exchange of vehicles, but when Phoenix began driving the Excursion, we wound up at a rather large gated complex that read Pearing Condominiums of Lincoln Park. I didn't ask any questions as Phoenix led me to his underworld.

The condo we entered was moderately furnished with dark green leather furniture against blond hardwood floors. There was a beautiful stone fireplace that I'm sure was great during Chicago's cold winters. While Phoenix talked on the phone, I looked around and noticed that there were two king-size bedrooms and a den with a poker table in the center, set with chips and other gaming items. I realized that this was Phoenix's home away from home.

I sat on the couch and waited for Phoenix to end his call.

He ended his call and placed a bottle of Grey Goose vodka and two glasses in front of us.

"I hope you don't expect me to drink that shit?"

"You punking out on me? You used to be able to go hard. What you need, some orange juice?"

"That would help."

"You want to know about the gambling, huh?"

"I want to know what the source is threatening to tell."

"Sasha, you know how competitive I am—that's why I play so hard. But dig this, when you've bought everything imaginable and some things that people can't even fathom, you go searching for something else."

I raised my eyebrows at him and leaned over to pour the vodka into the shot glasses. I passed him one.

He took the shot down. In turn I took one, and my throat felt like it was on fire. I quickly followed it with the orange juice.

"It started with the poker games. It was fun, the smell of money among peers who can bet for any amount. Expensive cigars and women who are there just for your pleasure. I mean real women, not them fuckin' groupies that be hanging around.

"Back when you were with me, I carried two, three thousand dollars. Now I carry no less than twenty. 'Cause there's always a game, in every city, an opportunity for a bet."

"Does that mean that your games are exclusive to athletes?"

"Hell, no. If you got the money, then you can go."

He lit a cigar, and I watched as the flames caught until it was fully lit. "It got to a point where basketball just wasn't enough."

The sting from another shot of the Grey Goose burned my throat.

It was time to stop bullshitting, so I asked, "How bad is it?"

"Once you get started, and you're winning, it's in your blood and you find yourself betting on anything. Man, this shit started out as a joke during a poker game, but one night I'm on the court busting my ass, and I realize just how much power I have to control the game, so just for kicks I bet on myself to see if I could really swing things a different way, and it worked. It was a whole new rush for me."

He stopped talking, just sat there in thought, his feet on the coffee table. He swallowed another shot. It was going to be a long night.

I kicked off my shoes and curled my legs under me on the couch. I knew that I couldn't take another shot of vodka, or I'd be drunk.

"Can one person actually control the game like that?"

"Shit, yeah. I do most of the scoring, don't I? It's not about who wins or loses, it's all about the point spread. Let's say somebody is betting ten thousand that the other team wins by eight points, favor Chicago. The underdog always gets the points. It's my job to make sure the point spread is not past ten even if we win."

I wasn't sure I understood how it worked, but what I did know was that he was definitely guilty of shaving points. "Who else is doing this, Phoenix?"

"You know I can't tell you that."

"How much does Crystal know, and better yet, what about that damn Mitchell?"

"Mitchell thinks he knows something, but he doesn't, just the regular gambling shit. And Crystal, she knows more than she should."

"This could bring down the NBA. How long have you been doing this point-shaving thing?"

"Too damn long. The real money, though, comes during the playoffs. Just last year alone I made over $3 million. The fucked-up part is that after a while the bets get bigger, and when you don't want to play, you wonder what will happen if you say no. So you're locked in."

"Do you think you're being blackmailed? Is that why this is happening?" I said, my speech a little slurred. Phoenix poured me another shot.

"I'm not sure, but I do believe it has something to do with those fucking diamonds."

"How so?"

"This guy that I play with was asking about them, saying they belonged to his people. I kept telling him I didn't have them. Then he stops asking, and all of a sudden this shit starts. He's a well-connected motherfucker, and I can't quite prove that it's him." He nodded his head. "LT has made a lot of money off me."

"One last question."

"What's that?"

"Do the diamonds belong to him?"

He pursed his lips, lowered his head, and mumbled, "You bet."

It didn't matter that I was drunk. I poured us both another shot. He rested his head against the back of the couch, his eyes closed, as he twirled the shot glass around in his hand. I was tempted to go to him.

"Phoenix."

"Yo."

"What do you want me to do?"

"Just ride with me on this one."

10

BALANCING ACT

September

Thursday evening Daddy called and suggested we have a big family dinner before his surgery on Wednesday. I unsuccessfully tried to convince him to make reservations, at a nice restaurant but he wasn't having it.

"Now, Sasha, you know your Daddy don't want no store-cooked food before he goes under the knife. I want something nice, you know, like on *Soul Food.*"

"Daddy, c'mon now. We don't have no Big Momma."

"We got Clara."

I felt a sting of jealousy, "Oh, so you'd rather Clara cook for you than me?"

"Sweetness, now you know better. I'm just saying she can take some of the weight off you and Deirdre, especially since I know y'all ain't gonna cook me no sweet Georgia ham."

"Daddy, it's not like you're dying."

"Yeah, but just in case, I wanna make sure I eat good before I check outta here."

"Please, Daddy, don't play like that."

"Does that mean I can tell the fellas they can stop by for dinner on Sunday?"

"Sure, Daddy, whatever you want."

I put in a call to Arshell to invite her up to Daddy's dinner.

"Sasha, where the hell you been?"

"Where've I been? You're the one who's never home when I call."

"Oh, yeah, you're probably right. So what's up?"

"Daddy's having his surgery next week, and he wants to have a big dinner on Sunday so I want you, Wayne, and the kids to come up."

"Good, but I'm not bringing Wayne."

"Why not?"

"I'll tell you all about it when I get up there. Plan on us being there on Saturday."

"What's going on?"

"Nothing I can talk about right now. Just have a bottle of that good-ass wine you and that banker been drinking, okay?"

By Friday, Deirdre and I had shopped enough to feed three families, which would probably be the required amount for the number of friends I was sure Daddy had invited. Every time I asked him who was coming, he'd say, "Just a few of the guys from the neighborhood."

Saturday evening the house was in a frenzy. We were

cleaning collard greens, steaming cabbage, and cutting up cheese for baked macaroni.

Arshell arrived with her twin boys, who were soon chasing Lil O and Jada throughout the house.

Jordan, who I'd also invited, had stopped by to drop off bags of ice and a few bottles of wine, something he could never seem to do without. Arshell was impressed with him but thought he was a little too dry for my taste.

At my house later that night, Arshell and I went downstairs to get comfortable over a bottle of wine after she'd settled her boys into my guest room.

"You blew me off a couple of weeks ago, and now you have my full attention. What's going on besides the menopause shit?"

"It's Wayne. Our marriage is done."

"Done? What do you mean? He just bought you that beautiful house."

"House or not, me and Wayne haven't had sex in months."

"Because of the menopause?"

"I'd like to believe that, but I just don't feel anything for him."

"Maybe you two should get some counseling. You just don't give up 'cause of the sex."

"Sasha, you know Wayne and I have been together since high school. There's just no way you can keep excitement in a marriage after all this time, and believe me, this transitioning stuff don't make it any better."

"Maybe the two of you need to take a vacation. You know, get away alone together."

"You're dreaming. That shit doesn't work in real life.

We probably wouldn't even know what to do alone together."

"For starters, you could get back to doing the nasty," I said, trying to lighten her mood.

"Not with this dry-ass pussy."

"Well then, get some of that KY Jelly shit."

"Seriously, I've tried to use that stuff, and Wayne just doesn't have the patience."

"You're telling me he's satisfied with not having sex?"

"He says sex isn't important, but it is, Sasha. You don't know what it's like when your husband turns his back on you. I love Wayne, but my body won't let me be a woman to him." She began to cry.

I kneeled in front of her chair and took her hands in mine.

"Oh, sweetie. We'll figure out something."

"I need to tell you something."

But before she could tell me, her cell phone rang. And hearing the voice of whoever it was on the other end put a smile back on her face. I knew that look, and it scared me. When she finished her call, I wasted no time confirming my suspicions.

"Arshell, are you cheating on Wayne? You can't go around laying up with other men just because of some damn menopause."

"I'm not laying up with anybody. He's just been somebody to talk to and hang out with."

"You've got a husband and three kids to hang out with."

"You don't get it, do you? You've been by yourself for so long, you can't imagine what it's like for me."

Her words hit a tender spot. Many times I wished I

had a husband and children to cater to. But as much as I wanted to understand her dilemma, I couldn't deny that this man was putting a smile on her face. If this was what menopause held for Arshell, then what the hell did it hold for me?

On Sunday afternoon Daddy's house was filled with a mix of aromas. Deirdre was forking the last pieces of fried chicken out of the deep fryer as Arshell stood at the stove stirring and thickening gravy for the cornbread-stuffed turkey. Hot buttered rolls that Clara had made from scratch sat on the dining-room table. At Daddy's request I'd baked a four-inch-deep lasagna with Italian sausage and meatballs. And Jordan brought the best dish of candied yams and apples I'd ever tasted. And yes, Clara baked Daddy a ham dripping with brown sugar and pineapples.

The last time I'd seen Daddy's house so full of life was when he'd had card games. I'd probably been about ten years old when I would play hostess for him and his friends. I'd serve them drinks and snacks, and they would give me tips.

I had to admit, though, that even with all the laughter, it was scary watching everyone eating, drinking, and talking trash. I prayed this wasn't some kind of sign that Daddy might not survive his surgery. He must've noticed me getting a little misty-eyed when he saw me standing against the wall, holding Jada. He came over, hugged us both, and said, "Ain't nothing gonna happen to your daddy, girl, so stop looking like you gonna cry."

No matter how much of a professional I was or how much money I made, Daddy was always able to make me feel like his little girl.

Clara was good for Daddy. I watched as she replenished Daddy's ice when it melted and served him "a little bit more gravy" before sitting down to eat her own food. She was the type of woman I imagined I could be to a deserving man. Daddy acted like he didn't even notice as he talked trash, cussing and laughing with his friends.

Listening to them warmed my spirit. They were so colorful in their conversation, they could've had their own television sitcom.

I took a quick break from all the hoopla and went upstairs to check my messages. Sitting in Daddy's recliner, I looked around the room and noticed that some of Clara's things had begun trickling in.

Lyor had phoned and invited me to dinner. Trent had called, too. "Hello, Sasha. I haven't heard from you since our brunch. Are you trying to tell me something?"

He just didn't get it—it wouldn't work—but I had to admit I enjoyed his persistence. Truth be told, I wasn't sure how I'd gotten myself caught up in such a sensuous dance of foreplay with all these men, but I couldn't deny that I was enjoying it.

But it was Jordan I wanted. And I would have him tonight. He was the one who would be dependable, the head I wanted to dent the pillow next to me, the underarms I wanted to smell. I knew that if I settled for Jordan, I would no longer have to be alone or anxious. My daydreaming was interrupted when I heard Arshell walking up the steps, calling my name.

Sitting down on the bed across from me, she said, "I didn't mean to lay all that on you last night, but I just need you to support me so I can get through this. I hope you're not too disappointed in me."

I could see that she needed me to approve of what she was doing, and even though I didn't, I kept that to myself. I sat next to her on the bed and put my arm around her shoulders. She was my best friend, right or wrong, I had to support her.

"Arshell, I love you. I just don't want you to get hurt. Who is this man? He must be someone special to take your attention from Wayne and the children."

"You're going to laugh when I tell you. He's certainly no Wayne when it comes to business. And he is special. But he's . . ."

"Don't tell me he's like fifteen years younger than you or anything like that."

"No, that's more your style. But seriously, he's really nice, but he is, uh, our mechanic."

"Your what?" I asked, while doubling over in laughter.

"All right, it's not that funny."

"Oh, hell yes, it is. I hope his hands and shit aren't dirty, 'cause you'll be going home smelling like oil and shit."

She playfully hit me on the arm. "You're getting a good laugh out of this, aren't you? Just wait till I give him some, then we'll see how greasy he is."

"Maybe he can grease up that dry pussy you been complaining about."

We laughed and talked until Jordan called up the steps to ask what all the noise was about.

Later that evening, after everyone had left and Daddy had gone to Clara's, Deirdre and I finished cleaning up. By ten o'clock I was tired but still ready for Jordan. I'd already told him I was taking him home with me, so he was more than ready.

After he showered, I followed behind him to get the

smell of food off me. Later I found him downstairs, where he'd already opened the bottle of Vin Santo wine I'd purchased for the occasion.

"Why don't you sit down and let me serve you?" he said, while removing a bowl of seedless grapes from the refrigerator.

I sat on the couch and watched as he uncorked the bottle.

"Where did you get the wine?" he asked.

"I wanted to surprise you. How'd I do?"

"A damn good choice. You know, you fixed a helluva meal today, girl. That means you'll make a good wife."

"That's what I'm aiming for," I answered, sliding off the couch to sit on the floor between his opened legs.

Handing me the glass of wine, he leaned over and kissed my shoulders. "This is nice, Sasha, real nice."

"What's that?"

"You know, me and you, us being together like this," he said, while his fingers pulled down the straps of my nightgown.

I plucked a grape and passed it over my head to him. I didn't answer, because I was anxious to see if Jordan Ashe could satisfy me.

"Why don't you put those hands to good use?" I asked, stretching out on the floor.

Kneeling in front of me, he took two grapes and with the palms of his hands rubbed one against each of my nipples. Pushing up on my elbows, I reached for the half-full bottle of wine and swallowed, allowing some of the liquid to run down my chin. There was no protest from Jordan that I was holding the bottle wrong or that I was warming its contents with my hands.

He caught the overflow of wine in the palm of his hand, then slid two of his wet and sticky fingers in my mouth. I glanced down between his legs. It was obvious he was ready.

Anxious to get inside me, he attempted to open my legs, but I placed my hands on his chest, pushing him away. "No, not yet." I plucked another grape from the vine, spread my legs, and slipped the grape inside me.

Jordan sat back and watched as I performed for him. I took the grape, now stained with my juices, from inside me and rubbed it against his lips. His tongue reached out and curled it into his mouth.

Jordan stroked himself, further lengthening and hardening his dick for me.

"You wanna get in here, don't you?" I asked, while feeding him the juices that ran down my fingers.

I grabbed his head with both hands and pulled him toward me. He opened his mouth, attempting to kiss me, but instead I tilted my head to the side, avoiding his lips. I gently pushed his head down, and he tried to stop to kiss my breasts, but I wasn't in the mood for that either, so I kept pushing until his tongue circled my navel.

"Please lemme give it to you, Sasha."

With that he pushed his tongue straight into me, far up inside, until he reached a spot that caused me to climax all over his mouth.

An inaudible sound was all I heard from him as he licked my clit and sucked at its now swollen lips.

He reached his fingers inside, opening me wide and burying his face deeper. I knew I'd come again.

"Fuck me, Jordan, this is what you've been waiting for."

All in one move, his lips, flavored with my juices, met

mine while his hand fumbled in an effort to ram his dick inside me.

"Sasha, oh, Sasha," he moaned between kisses, too weak to really ask for what he wanted. But instead of allowing him to mount me, I pushed him away until he was flat on his back.

I eased slowly down onto him. "Oh, my God, Sasha. Oh, my God, please, please," he cried out, his eyes wide, his face red.

He thrust his hips upward deep into the cavity of my essence. "Damn, you taking all this dick."

"Hold on, Jordan, hold on."

"Sasha, I can't. I can't hold on, I'm coming," and with that he let go, his body limp beneath mine.

Wednesday at 6:00 A.M., Owen, Daddy, and I arrived at the University of Pennsylvania Hospital. After signing his admission papers, and when his vital signs had been taken, his blood drawn, and he had donned a hospital gown, he was assigned a bed in the pre-op unit. All much too fast for me, but this was no time to get emotional.

Once Daddy was taken into surgery, Owen and I headed to the cafeteria, where over coffee we made small talk about work until two hours later Jerry found us. He assured us that everything had gone well and that Daddy was being moved into recovery.

Relieved that the surgery was over, I stepped outside to call the office. I checked my cell phone, where I had three messages, two from Phoenix and the other from Lyor. Before returning those calls, I phoned Jordan at the bank.

"Hi, Jordan."

"How'd it go? You sound a little frustrated."

"No, just tired. But everything's fine. Daddy's in recovery."

"Good, I knew he'd be okay. Hey, I didn't know you represented Phoenix Carter."

"You weren't much in the mood for talking the other night," I said, playfully.

"You're right, and I don't want to talk much tonight either."

"And what's happening tonight, Jordan?"

"Why don't you just plan on stopping by? I'm fixing some broiled flounder with a little stewed tomatoes and corn. Sound good to you?" I could hear in his voice that he wanted to see me as much as I wanted to see him.

"I'm excited."

"That's just how I want you. Whenever you get finished at the hospital, just come by."

No sooner had I dropped my cell phone back into my purse than it began to vibrate. It was Phoenix, going ballistic about losing everything he'd built up because of some bullshit and how he was going to take somebody's life.

"Phoenix, what the hell are you talking about?"

"Look, you gotta get down here. We gotta talk. Somebody went to see the commissioner."

"I thought you were supposed to meet with that guy?"

"I went to see him, and that motherfucker had already been up there, talking shit."

"Phoenix, you're not making sense. What happened with your meeting with LT?"

"I was set to meet with that bastard and was even thinking about giving him back them damn diamonds. But in the meantime he called the commissioner and the head of fucking NBA security, so I had to get my ass to New York."

"What happened in New York? You went by yourself?"

"Mitchell met me, and they said some guy went up to see them, talking about he can prove that I've been shaving fuckin' points. That's bullshit. Can't nobody prove shit."

"Has anything hit the papers yet?"

"No. He's supposedly promised not to say anything yet, but I need you to get down here tonight. We gotta talk, 'cause I'm gonna take somebody out."

"Your threatening to kill somebody over this damn cell phone is not helping the situation. Calm the hell down."

"How soon can you get down here?"

"Where are you?"

"Miami."

"Listen, Phoenix. I'm at the hospital right now. My father just had surgery, and I at least have to stay around till tomorrow. I'll fly out then."

"I'm sorry, Sasha. Is he all right?"

"He's fine, but it's you I'm worried about."

"I'll be all right. You go ahead and handle your father. I'll figure this shit out."

"Phoenix, stop it. I know you need me. Just give me a day."

"Yeah, all right."

By the time Daddy woke up, I was on my third cup of coffee and in full swing on the phone, handling work. I thought of canceling my dinner with Jordan but instead decided to go home and pack a bag so that I could travel directly from Jordan's house to Miami.

As soon as I walked into the house, my phone rang.

"I finally caught up with you. I don't understand why a brother has to track you down," Trent said as I answered the phone.

"Trent, I'm sorry I haven't gotten back to you. Daddy had his surgery today."

"Oh, baby, he's all right, isn't he?"

"Yes, he's good."

"You sure you don't need me to come down there?"

Laughing, I said, "No, I'm fine."

"I'm here for you. You know that, right?"

"Yes. But I don't know why."

"We'll talk about that when you get some time."

On the way to Jordan's house I phoned Arshell for advice. I needed to make sense out of Trent's behavior.

"How's things going down there?"

"Not too good today," Arshell mumbled, seeming distracted.

"What's wrong?"

"I've been in bed all day. I just feel miserable, but enough about me. How's your father?"

"He's fine. Where's Wayne?"

"He went out Ohio to speak at some conference or something. He'll be back Saturday morning."

My friend sounded distressed, and I wanted to go to her, but I was on my way to Jordan's, and Phoenix needed me, too.

"Where are you, still at the hospital?"

"No, I'm on my way to Jordan's, and then in the morning I'm off to Miami, but I want to come down there."

"It's no biggie. I'll get through this."

"What about your friend, the mechanic?"

"I've just finished talking to him."

I parked in front of Jordan's house. "Arshell, I love you."

"I love you, too. Now go see your man and call me when you get to Miami. Be careful down there with Phoenix."

Jordan was just putting the finishing touches on his meal. When I arrived, he had the table set for us, and the wine was already poured.

"You look good for someone who's been at the hospital all day."

"You smell good, just like fish."

"Let's eat. I'm starved."

We never made it to dessert. By the time I had my second glass of wine, all I wanted was him. So rather than engage in conversation about the bank, I made him take me over the back of the dining-room chair.

Daddy was going to be in the hospital for four days. When I returned to the hospital the following morning, there was barely any space for me in his room, it was so full of visitors. Even the nurses spent more time with him then necessary, and he enjoyed all the attention, especially the home-cooked food that Clara brought. I sat quietly, watching him in his glory, until he asked me when I was going back to work.

"Monday, but Phoenix has some stuff going on, so I may have to fly down to Miami first."

"Sasha, girl, take your butt back to work. I'm fine."

I arrived in Miami on Thursday night, and this time I was picked up by Trey in a Cadillac Escalade and taken to the Tides Hotel on Ocean Drive. I was glad to be in Florida's ninety-degree heat, since Philly's weather had been so unpredictable lately.

Phoenix had arranged for me to have breakfast with his wife, Crystal, in the morning. I just hoped that his plans didn't interfere with my plans to steal some time on the beach. I wasn't sure why Crystal and I were meeting, but Phoenix said she had some concerns about what was "happening" with him. My instincts told me they had more to do with Phoenix and me working together again.

Around ten-thirty that night there was a knock on my hotel door. Opening it, I found Phoenix in a powder-blue Polo shirt and jeans, diamonds dripping from his neck, wrists, and fingers.

Shaking my head at his attire, I said, "I'm impressed."

"Yo, Sasha, this is South Beach—you can be whatever you want down here. You gotta remember, I'm still young, and right now I don't give a fuck what people think."

"I see," I responded, knowing that was far from the truth.

"How's your daddy doing?" he asked as he sat on the king-size bed, changing channels with the remote.

"He's good. I just finished talking to him, and he told me to tell you hello."

He'd obviously found something of interest on television, because he was arranging the bed pillows and propping them up behind him. "Yeah, well, I have something I want to send him."

"He has everything he needs."

"We'll see about that."

I wasn't going to argue with him; I knew Daddy would enjoy bragging to his friends that he'd received a get-well present from the great Phoenix Carter.

Heading toward the bathroom, I could feel Phoenix watching me. "When the hell did your ass fill out like that?" he asked, ogling the Diesel skirt and white halter top I wore.

"It's all the good loving I'm getting." I replied coyly, bending over to adjust my lace-up sandals around my calves.

"Damn, Sasha. I see I'm not the only one iced out!" he said as I hooked the latch on my tennis bracelet.

"Where are we going?"

"I got a little place I'm gonna take you to."

"Sounds interesting."

I was trying to keep up with Phoenix's long strides through the crowded hotel lobby when a local reporter spotted us and rushed over, notebook in hand.

"Excuse me, Mr. Carter. Will you be doing any gambling while you're in Miami?"

"I don't know. Is it legal down here?"

I stepped between Phoenix and the reporter, giving Trey, who was waiting at the revolving door, the opportunity to get Phoenix outside. Turning to the reporter, I said, "Mr. Carter won't be speaking with the press this evening."

"And you are?" the reporter asked, pissed that Phoenix had dodged him.

"Sasha Borianni, Mr. Carter's publicist," I stated, pushing one of my cards between the pages of his black notebook.

When I got outside, it wasn't hard for me to spot Phoenix sitting in the driver's seat of a silver convertible Bentley. I climbed in the passenger's side.

"How did they know you were here? Are you staying in this hotel?"

"Sasha, they know everything except where we're going tonight."

Pushing a button on the steering wheel, he sent music through the air at an astronomical decibel. Over the loud music I asked, "What's up for tomorrow?"

"Don't worry. I got it all covered."

"What time is our meeting? I scheduled my flight for six o'clock."

"After your little breakfast with my wife, I'll pick you up, and we'll go from there."

Once again, Phoenix had totally disregarded my plans.

Instead of going to some out-of-the-way restaurant, we traveled forty-five minutes to a gated community without a name posted on the gate. Stretching his long arm across the door, Phoenix pushed a few buttons on the security panel, and the gates slowly opened. Trees and lush landscapes separated each of the giant homes. We continued along the main road to what appeared to be a dead end and then turned onto a narrow lane leading to an almost all-glass house. The winding driveway took us toward the front door, where we were met by two valets, one at Phoenix's door and the other at mine, ready to assist us.

My first thought was that someone from the music industry owned this house, judging by the flashiness of the sprawling mansion and the way music seemed to be pumping from the sky. However, I was surprised when Guiliana Valentine, a hot new designer from Milan, greeted Phoenix. Phoenix told me she wanted him to do some modeling work.

Among all the people in their designer separates, all logoed up and loaded with flashy jewelry, I felt underdressed. I recognized plenty of faces but couldn't recall the names, so I floated around and allowed myself to be introduced by Phoenix.

Standing on the veranda at the back of the house, Guiliana approached me and asked, "Are you enjoying the party?"

"Yes. The party is great, and your home is beautiful."

"Tell me, who else do you represent?"

"Most of my clients are corporate. I only work with celebrities like Phoenix on a select basis, as they can be very demanding."

As we stood there talking, a very rotund, tanned gentleman who looked to be in his late fifties walked up and kissed Guiliana on the mouth. Before she could introduce us, he grabbed my hand and kissed me on the cheek.

"Harry Bowen, this is Sasha Borianni."

I was dumbstruck but anxious to see if there would be any recognition when he heard my name. There should—I'd been calling repeatedly, trying to get a contract to do publicity for his company, Bowen Entertainment.

"You're the young lady who's been trying to get an appointment with me?"

"Yes, that would be me. I recall your telling me to give you a call the next time I was in L.A."

"Is that so? And who, might I ask, are you here with?"

"Harry, my dear, she belongs to Phoenix."

"I had no idea. Why didn't you tell somebody that when you phoned my office? Come, tell me what you're proposing to do for Bowen Entertainment."

We walked along the stone paving past a steaming hot tub and softly lit pool as I explained how I wanted to handle the PR for the upcoming movie he'd be filming in Philadelphia. Before I could finish my pitch, Phoenix caught up with us.

"Yo, Harry, what you doing? Trying to steal my girl?" I could tell Phoenix had had a few drinks.

"I was just telling the sexy Ms. Sasha Borianni that I'll sign her up to do whatever she's good at."

Pulling me from Harry's arm to his, Phoenix answered, "She's good at everything."

And just like that, I got the deal with Harry Bowen.

By the time I got back to my room, it was daybreak. I stripped off clothes that felt like glue, just a little drunk. I didn't even take the time to wash the makeup off my face or check messages. Before I could fall asleep, the hotel phone rang.

"So have you been enjoying Miami to the wee hours?"

"Lyor? How'd you know I was in Miami?"

"Cute little miniskirt you were wearing tonight. How come I've never seen you dressed like that in Philadelphia?"

I took my face out of the pillow. "Where are you?"

"Little did you know, but I was sitting at the lobby bar when you left tonight with your Mr. Carter."

"You were? Why didn't you say something?"

"You get some rest, and I'll give you a call in the morning."

Rather than try to figure out where he was or wasn't, I turned over and went back to sleep.

In what seemed like just an hour, the phone rang again, my wake-up call. I could barely move because of a throbbing headache on the left side of my head. I knew it was from too much alcohol and not enough sleep. How the hell was I going to be lucid enough to face Crystal?

I made it to the bathroom and rummaged through my toiletries until I found some Excedrin. I downed two caplets, and even though it wasn't a good idea, I climbed back into bed to give myself another fifteen minutes of rest.

I jumped up at eight o'clock. The pounding in my head had subsided. I dragged myself to the shower, slipped on a spaghetti-strap sundress and a pair of ankle-wrap sandals, and applied a little makeup to hide the bags under my eyes. I was set to go when the phone rang. Mrs. Crystal Carter was waiting poolside for me.

Arriving at the entrance to the outdoor pool, I spotted Crystal lounging poolside at a shaded table. She wore a white sleeveless dress against her bronzed skin. She'd filled out some from the skinny nineteen-year-old girl she was when I first met her.

"Good morning, Crystal. I'm so sorry I'm late."

"I just arrived," she said, giving me the kind of hug where only our arms touched.

"You look great," I said, hoping my compliment would melt some of the ice.

"Um, so do you."

We ordered breakfast, which for me was just a bagel and coffee. My stomach couldn't handle much more. She ordered yogurt topped with fruit.

She started right in. "What brings you to Miami? I mean, I know you're trying to help Phoenix work through this little thing, but I didn't expect you'd be down here for a visit."

My head suddenly began to clear up—either from the caffeine or my awareness that she was trying to run game on me.

"I'm down here for a meeting with your husband." I yawned into my hand.

"I'm sorry, Sasha. Am I boring you, or did you have a late night?"

This bitch, I thought to myself.

"I'm going to be straight up with you. Sasha, there's no pretending like I'm glad you're back in Phoenix's life. But know this, if you're going to be around, it better be worth it."

We stopped talking while the waiter set our food in front of us.

"I'm not sure I understand." But maybe I did. Maybe Crystal hadn't been as innocent as I'd thought. Maybe she knew I had an affair with her husband back then. I took a much-needed sip of my coffee before continuing. "Crystal, I've been hired to help your husband keep his image intact amid all these allegations. No more, no less."

She picked at her fruit and said, "That's bullshit and we both know it. But what you should know is that I am way over Phoenix's accomplishments *and* his indiscretions. My only concern is for me and my children, that we don't lose our position among our peers or our financial status."

"We both know that your husband is a rich, powerful, and well-known man who could've hired any firm in the country, but obviously he's chosen Platinum Images."

"Or is it just Sasha Borianni he's chosen?"

"Crystal, why did you really want to meet with me?"

"You haven't figured that out yet? Sasha, if I find out you're fucking my husband, I promise it'll be your image you'll find yourself protecting."

I carefully gathered my thoughts as I looked over her sparkling diamonds and designer clothes. She should be glad that I wasn't the old Sasha, or the bullshit she was displaying would only have given me cause to go fuck Phoenix on the next opportunity and make sure she found out.

I pulled off my sunglasses, leaned back in my chair. "Crystal, you've made your concerns for your family and for who *your* husband chooses to fuck very clear, but there's no need to worry. I've always taken care of your husband, which in turns means I've always taken care of you, too. Now if that's all you have, then I have to go."

"Go if you want, but remember what I said."

I could've sworn I heard her mumble the word *bitch* at the end of that sentence, but it didn't matter. I returned to my hotel room and called the office to check with Michael.

"Hey, Michael. What's going on there?"

"There's a message here that you should find interesting."

"What's that?"

"It looks like Harry Bowen's office called, and he's inviting you to L.A. to fine-tune your deal."

"What? Already?"

"I wasn't aware that you'd even had a real conversation with him yet."

"I met him at a party last night with Phoenix. Listen, tell Kendra to call his office and schedule my trip out there. I want to get this done before he changes his mind. Also, ask her to fax me one of our contracts here to the hotel, so I can mark it up on the plane. Anything else?"

"I'll fax it. Kendra's in a meeting with Tiffany right now. You might've heard of Marcus Harris, a former Steelers quarterback who ended up in a wheelchair."

"Vaguely."

"Well, it turns out that Mr. Harris is interested in starting a Youth-at-Risk Football Camp, for which he already has several major sponsors, but he'd like our help in supporting this endeavor. This might be a big one, and Kendra's going to work with Tiffany on it."

"Good, good. I'll be back in Philly tomorrow, and we can get caught up at Monday's staff meeting. Tell Tiffany and Kendra I said good luck."

Looking at my watch I saw that it was nearing eleven-thirty and I was dying to get to the beach. I changed into the swimsuit I'd packed—a little too tight around the ass, but it would have to do—found a spot by myself on the beach, and spread out a clean hotel towel for a little relaxation.

At three o'clock I was waiting outside the hotel for Phoenix to pick me up. Even though he appeared to be alone, I knew that Trey had followed in the Escalade.

"Damn, you look good. You got black as shit."

"Well, I got a little too black. My skin is burned and sore as hell."

We rode along Collins Avenue and turned into the Shops at Bal Harbour. When the valet took his keys, I asked, "Phoenix, why are we at the mall? I thought we were having a meeting. You need to be getting prepared for this media bulldozing, not shopping."

"You're right. We are meeting, you and me, here at the mall."

"Oh, this is bullshit. I have a business to run. I'm not your personal assistant anymore," I said, walking away from him.

He caught up to me as I entered the doors of Neiman's.

"Listen, this is the best place for us to talk. I don't want to be looking out for no damn reporters."

And that's what we did. We sat at a café inside the mall near the pond and talked for two hours, surprisingly, without any interruptions.

"Sasha, there are two things going on here, and I think both are connected. I met with LT last night, and I told him once again that I didn't have his brother's diamonds. I also told him that I knew someone, who for now remains nameless, at least to me, had gone to the commissioner. But I knew it was him, or he'd paid somebody to do it for him."

"How'd you figure that out?"

"Listen, the head of security laid it out for me. They know everything. LT was going to blackmail me anyway. Sasha, I'm sorry I had to involve you in this thing, but I didn't have a choice back then. Your house was the only place where I knew they'd be safe."

"When was the last time you talked to LT?"

"A few hours ago."

"Did you tell him you were returning them?"

"I told him I might be able to put him touch with someone, for a fee."

"What did the commissioner say during your meeting?"

"He wants to know who else is involved, any other players, how much money is involved. I didn't give up the tapes on anyone, but if I don't squash this, my career is fucked."

"What are you going to do about the diamonds?"

"After I get them out your house, I'll have someone handle it from there. In the meantime I have to get this gambling in check. I can't get kicked out of the NBA, I wouldn't be able to handle that."

"Phoenix, this is all too much for me to take in in one afternoon." I didn't mention it to Phoenix, but I wondered if Lyor could help out.

I'd missed my flight back to Philly on Friday night, so I called Jordan to tell him that I'd fly out in the morning and lay down to take a nap, hoping that all this information would settle somewhere in my head and I would wake up with a plan. But before I could nod off, the hotel room phone rang.

"You're still here."

I was happy to hear Lyor's voice. "Don't tell me you're a stalker."

"You're a woman who needs watching. Do you have to work tonight?"

"Wait a minute, Lyor. Are you still in Miami?"

"Yes, and I would like to have an early dinner with you."

"I would, but I was just getting ready to lie down for a little while. Can we do it later?"

"Sure. Why don't I call you around seven? Would that give you enough time for beauty rest?"

When I woke up it was after seven, and Lyor hadn't called. While I was in the shower my cell phone rang, and he left a message that he'd be in the lobby waiting for me, well tanned in white pants and shirt.

We had dinner at a very loud Moroccan restaurant, where I found it a relief to drink some Paradis, since I was always drinking wine with Jordan.

"How long will you be in Miami?" he asked.

"I'm going back tomorrow. My vacation is over, and I'm due back in the office on Monday."

"What a shame. I was going to suggest you go up to Naples with me for the greyhound races. Who knows, you could have beginner's luck and win a bundle."

Little did Lyor know, but gambling was the furthest thing from my mind, especially with the trouble Phoenix was in.

"Can I get a rain check?"

"You can get anything you want from me." Lyor's eyes were getting a little glassy, and I wondered if maybe his third drink was going to his head. But I liked seeing him like this. He was relaxed.

"Since you won't go to Naples with me, then let's hang out a little."

"I'm up for it."

Lyor was very familiar with the Miami party scene. We went from one club to another, and as I suspected, he wasn't a very good dancer. We had a good time buying drinks for people, talking trash while he made sure his hands were always touching some part of my body. The height of the night was when he convinced me to go to a strip club.

We arrived at the smoky, high-class gentleman's club around three in the morning. I was surprised that there were almost as many women as there were men. I had to admit his constant touching and whispering suggestive remarks in my ear while the women danced on stage aroused me.

I excused myself to go the ladies' room, and when I returned Lyor had a surprise for me. He signaled to a Hispanic woman—beautiful, slender, clad in only a G-string, her golden breasts perfectly mounted on her chest. She began circling me, talking in Spanish. I looked at Lyor to ask what the hell was going on, but he was standing back against the wall, watching me.

I couldn't believe I was letting this woman get so close to me. Her body moved and her ass jiggled when she bent over to spread her cheeks. I could easily smell her womanly scent. When she turned to face me, her nipples brushed against my face, tempting me to reach out and touch them. I wondered where she'd learned to slither like a snake, all around me. I was in a trance until Lyor came over, put a fifty-dollar bill in my hand, and whispered in my ear, "Put it inside her G-string."

I didn't even look at him, just took the money. She brought her pussy, absent of all hair, close to my face. I pulled the G-string away from her body and placed the bill in there. With that, my panties were soaked. In response there was clapping and shouts from everyone in the room. Lyor laughed and said into my ear, "I think you enjoyed that."

"Now I know why men come here. These women are unbelievable."

"Here, have a fresh drink. You look like you need some fresh air; let's go down to the beach."

We took our drinks and went outside. The ocean air felt good against my clammy skin. My own thong was soaked, and I knew that if Lyor wanted me, I was all his.

He led me toward the beach, where I kicked off my sandals and walked along the edge of the ocean, Lyor following behind me. I felt free, as if there was nothing I couldn't do. Lyor came up behind me and put his arms around my waist. We stood swaying together as he untied the front of my dress and unhooked my bra, his hands traveling across my breasts. I was hoping he'd take me right there on the almost empty beach, where only other lovers strolled. His hands moved from my breasts to the cheeks of my ass, gently squeezing them, all while he kissed the nape of my neck. I wanted to turn around, but he wouldn't let me, he just held me in front of him until my knees began to buckle. He turned me around and sucked my tongue deep into his mouth.

He spoke into my ear, his tongue tracing its lobe. "Sasha, you're beautiful. You were so sexy with that woman. I wanted to fuck you right there in front of all those people."

"Why not do it now, Lyor, right here?"

"No, you're not ready for me yet," he said, his fingers running up and down the length of my pussy.

"Lyor, I am, please." I couldn't believe I was begging him, this white man, to fuck me right here on the beach in front of other lovers. He knelt in front of me, put his head under my dress. A couple walked by and nodded. I couldn't have cared less.

He was so good at what he did that I never wanted him to stop. I held onto his curly head, and, shaking, he grabbed me as I fell to my knees onto the wet sand. He pulled off what was left of my dress, and lifted my legs over his shoulders, and there on the beach, with the sun sitting on the water, Lyor ate everything that belonged to me.

11

ROLLING THE DICE

I slept the entire two-hour flight back to Philly, still numb between my legs and able to feel the pressure of Lyor's mouth. Jordan waited for me at baggage claim.

"Hey, gorgeous. You look awesome, you must've needed that trip. I can't wait to get you home," he said, giving me a wet kiss on the mouth. "You seem a little tired."

"I shouldn't be. I slept the entire flight."

"I know just what you need."

Jordan was full of chatter on the ride to my house, so I knew there would be no way I could tell him good night at the door. I let him rattle on, asking about my work for Phoenix and if I got to meet any *cool* people. I told him enough to make him think my trip was fun. I *had* missed him. Even though I'd been pulled under by Lyor's loving mouth, I knew Jordan would be eagerly waiting for me, and I really did enjoy spending time with him.

"Listen, I want to invite you somewhere with me."

"Church again?"

"Nope," he said, reaching over to massage my sore thighs. "The Philadelphia Black Bankers Association is throwing their Annual Bankers Ball in two weeks, and I'd like for my best girl to accompany me."

"Jordan, that's nice. I'd be happy to go."

"I'm warning you it's going to be pretty stuffy, but I have a trade-off for you."

"I like the sound of that. What's the trade?"

"I'll pick up the tab for whatever you choose to wear if you'll promise to be the belle of the ball."

"A new outfit always works for me," I said, reaching over to hold his hand.

Owen had taken care of bringing my mail into the house, so there was a pile of it on the kitchen table. I called Daddy as soon as Jordan and I got into the house. He sounded really good and told me to stop by during the week for dinner.

"I should take a shower."

"No, stay just like that. I'll take care of you," Jordan said, tossing my locks around my head.

I plopped down on the couch and watched Jordan pour two glasses of champagne that he'd brought with him. I'd drunk too much over the weekend, so I knew my body couldn't take another drop of that volatile stuff.

"Are we celebrating something?"

"Oh, just us. I missed you over these last few days."

"I've missed you, too," I said, propping my feet up on him as he sat at the other end of the couch.

"Sit over here with me," he said.

He tickled me around my navel, which he knew drove me crazy.

"Take it easy, Jordan," I said as he pulled one of my breasts from underneath the thin white linen dress I was wearing.

Aroused by the tan Miami's sun had put on my body, he said, "Sasha, I have to have you right now."

I didn't know where I was going to get the energy.

"But first I want to ask you something. Seriously," he said.

"What's that?" I asked, annoyed that he wanted to change the mood.

"I know it's only been about six months, and we don't get to spend much time together because of our schedules, but I am most certain that I want you to be my woman. I want you to always know that you don't need to look anywhere else to have your needs met."

What was I supposed to say to him? That it was too late, that I'd let Lyor ravish me on a public beach? Could I possibly put out the fire that had already begun between us? I looked down at Jordan, his head in my lap, and I wanted to love him.

"What do you say?" He leaned forward and took my breast into his mouth.

"Take me like I'm already your woman."

For the first time in years I had a man. What had happened between Lyor and me in Miami wouldn't happen again. I'd promised myself that I would be faithful to Jordan.

Monday morning's staff meeting was hectic. By midafternoon I was back into the swing of things when the phone rang. It was an excited Pastor Price, who I hadn't heard from in a few weeks, telling me that he'd won the presidency. I suggested we meet over the next two weeks to prepare him for the Baptist Convention and his taking over the helm.

Lyor called two days later. Just as I was ready to give him the spiel about how we had to cut things off, he told me that he had a lucrative business offer for me and asked if I could meet him at his place for dinner. Rather than tell him about my decision over the phone, I decided to hear his offer first.

When I arrived at his apartment, I was surprised to find that he'd finished furnishing it. Everything was decorated in pastel colors, and his new cream leather furniture reminded me somehow of Miami. His apartment revealed his personal side as I watched him pointing out his collection of fine watches, family pictures, his precious five orchid plants that he'd had for two years, and the closet that held dozens of shoes.

"I hope you don't mind that I didn't cook myself, but I did help," he said, referring to the spread of catered food on his dining room table.

"I bet. What are we having?"

"How does fish sound?"

"Any fish sounds good, as long as it's not gefilte fish."

"Very funny. You'll be glad to know we'll be having salmon tonight."

I watched his mouth as we ate, remembering the pleasure that it had given me. Before I got carried away with myself, I asked him about the business he'd mentioned on the phone.

"I think I have some good news for you and this publicity business you love so much."

"I'm listening."

"I think I can get you the waterfront account."

"You think?" I didn't want to get too excited.

"I *know,* and as a matter of fact, it's already yours."

"Let me make sure I'm hearing you correctly. You're saying that I am the lead PR firm on the waterfront project."

"It is no longer the waterfront project. It's been named the Panache Casino and Hotel Complex. Your first meeting with the board of directors is scheduled for a month from now, and I've already told them to expect you."

This was not the time to hold back my excitement and gratitude, nor the time to tell him about Jordan. "Lyor, I don't know what to say. I had no idea you were going to do this for me."

"I told you when we first met you that I might have some business for you."

"You don't know how bad I've been wanting this opportunity."

"Now you have it. So make me proud and show those white boys what you can really do. I have no doubt that you will bring a lot to that table."

"I don't know how to thank you."

"You thanked me in Miami."

During dinner we talked like old friends about our lives and growing up, him in Long Island and me in Philadelphia. When he brought up his family's jewelry business, I thought about the diamonds in my safe. I asked him about the value of marquis and round diamonds and how a person would go about selling them on the black market, telling him that my interest in diamonds came from a television show I saw recently.

By the time we made it to the couch, it was pouring

rain outside. I could barely see the lights from the bridge, much less Philly's skyline. Lyor slouched down on the couch with the remote in one hand and his cat, Cashmere, in the other. I got comfortable, too, taking off my shoes and putting my feet in his lap. He put down the cat and pulled me over to him.

"You shouldn't go home in this weather. Why don't you sleep in my bed tonight, and I'll take the couch?"

"That's probably not a bad idea," I said. Jordan was out of town on business and wouldn't miss me. The fact that Lyor hadn't mentioned sex was disappointing, but I was too excited about Panache Casino to care—in the end it was all about business.

I left Lyor's apartment early the next morning so I could go home and change for work. On my car phone I had two messages from Arshell, who wanted me to call her back at a number I wasn't familiar with.

After dialing the number, I was surprised to hear a man's voice on the answering machine. When I began to leave a message, Arshell spoke into the phone.

"Arshell, what's going on? Where are you?"

"I'm at my friend's house. Listen, I need your help. I want to get away for a little bit, and I told Wayne that I was going with you on one of your business trips."

"Why'd you do that?"

"Sasha, please, please don't do this. Just tell me you'll help me out. Aren't you going somewhere soon?"

I tried to think fast. "I'm going to the Baptist Convention in Connecticut. You could meet me there. Are you sure about this?"

"Oh, I love you so much. Thank you. I'm going to call you tomorrow when Wayne leaves for work, and you can tell me where I should stay and all that stuff. I promise, Sasha, I'll never ask you to do this again."

After work that evening I stopped by Daddy's house to find out how his post-op checkup had gone. According to Daddy, everything had gone fine.

Thursday afternoon Jordan kept calling my office to talk about the Banker's Ball being held that evening at the Marriott. I couldn't figure out what he was so damn nervous about. He went to these things all the time, so maybe he was nervous because he'd be accepting an award for his work at Carson S&L. But my female intuition told me that there was another woman involved, possibly his ex-girlfriend he'd told me about who also worked in the banking industry. It didn't matter. I would be the one on his arm, wearing the fifteen-hundred-dollar dress he'd bought me.

I left work early and went into the city to meet Jordan at his house. He was eagerly waiting when I arrived. We had to be there at seven, so we didn't have time to make love, as I'd suggested as a way of calming him down. He'd gone all out and rented a limousine for the occasion, even though the hotel was only ten blocks from his house. But this was his big night; he was receiving an award for being one of the banking industry's Top Twenty People to Watch.

On the ride over I told Jordan about my being offered the PR campaign for the waterfront Panache Casino and Hotel. He was ecstatic, practically begging me to let his bank be involved, no matter how small a role it played.

The hotel lobby was filled with men in black tuxes and women in long black dresses. I knew I would stand out in the crowd. At Jordan's request to be different and liven up this boring crew, I wore a red vintage Ralph Lauren dress. His strategy worked; I was the only one among the women who'd dared to be different.

Inside, Jordan headed toward the bar, where he got us two glasses of their best wine. I put on my best corporate smile, realizing that the room, mostly filled with men, held potential business for Platinum Images. Before we took our seats, a woman whose breasts were too big for her skinny body slithered over to us. Miss Skin-and-Bones was on the arm of a not-so-handsome man whose tux looked like he'd rented it just that morning. My instincts told me that he was her replacement for Jordan Ashe.

"Sasha Borianni," Jordan said, gesturing toward me, "this is Beverly Longford, regional manager of Bostonian Savings." I had no idea why he felt I needed to know her title.

"Nice to meet you, Sasha," she said, reaching her skinny arm out to shake my hand, fingers only. I looked at her date to indicate that she hadn't introduced him. Looking at Jordan, she said, "And this is my friend Gregory." Poor Gregory was probably her cousin who she'd dragged to this event.

Jordan's hand tightened around mine as Beverly continued, "Jordan, I wasn't expecting *you* of all people to come with a date."

"I'm not sure if you know, but Sasha is the CEO of Platinum Images. She's part of the reason I'm receiving this award tonight. She's done a lot for the bank."

I wanted so bad to tell her what I'd done for him personally, but instead I decided to enjoy the little game the two of them were playing.

"How's your grandmother doing, Jordan?" Beverly asked. "Did she take her trip down to South Carolina this summer?"

He looked at me before answering, perhaps wondering if I cared that she was letting me know how familiar she was with him. Poor Jordan had no idea that I was a pro at this, and this woman, this girl, who was probably no more than twenty-nine, had no idea who she was fucking with.

"Grandma is fine. How's business at Bostonian?"

They took the conversation into the realm of banking, throwing around financial jargon to purposely exclude me. Gregory was paying them no attention, in a world of his own. I turned to look at Jordan, who was starting to look like a bobble-head doll in the back of somebody's car. That's when I noticed he had a small boogie hanging on one of the hairs from his left nostril, making his awkward display even more comical.

When Beverly and Gregory finally walked away, Jordan's face clearly showed his relief.

I didn't even want to hear him stutter an excuse. "It doesn't matter. But I should tell you that while you were standing there salivating over Beverly, you had a little flying boogie," I said, pointing at his nose. Poor Jordan's face turned a shade somewhere between orange and red as he quickly headed off to the men's room.

The rest of the night was uneventful as Jordan graciously accepted his award. Beverly was the first one to offer a standing ovation. Poor thing. I'd collected about ten business cards from men Jordan introduced me to and felt Beverly watching every move we made.

It was after twelve when we left. Jordan was quiet on

the short ride back to his house, and once we got inside, I asked him about Beverly.

"Was that the ex-girlfriend I met tonight?"

"Who? Beverly?"

"I think she was the only one you were drooling over."

"Sasha, I don't drool over anybody but you."

"I think you'll have to convince me of that."

"Come here, and I will."

Grabbing me by the waist, he pulled me toward him, planting kisses all over my face.

"I better not catch you drooling over no other woman except Sasha Borianni. You hear me?"

After we made love that night, we lay in bed talking about the things we wanted in life and the future we could have together. As I drifted off to sleep, I prayed that I could love Jordan.

12

PERSONAL TRIPS

October

The following week Kendra and I left for the Baptist Convention in Hartford, Connecticut. I'd told her that my girlfriend Arshell was coming up, and that she would be sharing a room with me. Only I knew that this was a planned rendezvous for Arshell and her mechanic lover.

During the past two weeks Pastor and I had prepared for the convention, which would have at least twenty thousand people in attendance. I didn't plan to linger at the convention. Once Pastor Price was named the incumbent president, I planned to return to Philly, then drive down to Solomon's Island, Maryland, to meet Jordan, who'd been dying to show me his boat, *Red Sage.* I was curious to see just what kind of sailor he was.

During our downtime Kendra and I walked the convention floor, which was filled with vendors, selling everything from Bibles to men's crocodile shoes. The hats the women attendees wore were unmatched by anything I'd ever seen in church. They sported colors and sizes that went with everything they wore. I spotted ministers pulling out wads of money like drug dealers. Every day there was a designated color that the men, women, and ministers adhered to. The ministers' suits ranged from finely tailored business suits to loud and gaudy gigolo getups. Had I not known better, I would've thought I'd walked into a pimp convention. I'd never seen anything like it.

I was in my hotel room, working on the contract for the Panache business, when Arshell arrived. Before answering her knock, I told myself that I'd be able to handle seeing Arshell and her mechanic. He was handsome in a country sort of way and used humor to get through our uncomfortable introduction. Arshell was giddy, and seeing that we needed to talk, he excused himself and left for his room to get unpacked.

"This is the man you've been sneaking around with?"

"Sasha, don't make it sound so bad."

"I should be the last person to judge anybody, but I love you and I love Wayne and the kids, and I just don't want to see any—" Arshell didn't let me finish.

"Nothing's going to happen with me and Wayne. Hell, we're getting along better now. My mechanic helps take the edge off all this menopausal shit."

"Whatever you say, Arshell, just don't screw up your home. Listen, I need to tell you something in the strictest confidence."

She looked at me as I dared to question her confidence.

"I think I've gotten in over my head with Phoenix."

"What do you mean? You're not fucking him again, are you?"

"Hell, no. This is worse, or maybe . . . I don't know. Remember those diamonds in my house?"

"Yes."

"Well, someone is asking for them back, and Phoenix doesn't want to give them up. He thinks this same someone is the person who's talking all this shit on him in the press."

"I haven't heard anything lately."

"I know, but we're thinking that, now the season has started, the shit is going to hit the fan."

"Sasha, when are you going to learn to stop helping him out of every jam he gets himself in? You tell that nigga to get that shit outta your house."

"I know. But I thought this was a clean-cut business deal where I could make a few thousand bucks."

"When are you gonna learn that it's all about Phoenix? Now, tell me the truth—have you fucked him yet?"

"Hell, no, and I'm not going to. Like I told you, I've committed myself to Jordan."

"And what about that rich Jew boy?"

"You mean Lyor?"

"Yes, Lyor. Isn't he the one that ate you up on the beach?"

"Girl, you're crazy. I haven't been with him like that since that night. But he did give me a great piece of business."

"What business is it that you couldn't get on your own?"

"The waterfront project, the new Panache Casino and Hotel."

"Oh, shit, that is big. Maybe you should let him eat you up again."

We laughed about it, but I knew I had to stay away from Lyor. I wanted to be one man's woman this time around.

After handling the media at Pastor's convention, I stopped in Philly to get a fresh bag of clothes, then took off down I-95 toward Solomon's Island. The drive took three hours, and when I arrived at the dock where his boat was parked, I learned that when Jordan took an interest in something, he went all the way.

Jordan stood on the deck, waving at me. He was dressed in a blue shirt with little white sailboats all over it, white shorts, and a pair of Docksiders. He helped me onto the twenty-nine-foot Bayliner and gave me a grand tour.

After freshening up, we decided to go out to dinner. Jordan selected an outdoor seafood restaurant where he taught me how to eat oysters—his point being that they were supposed to be an aphrodisiac.

I was waiting for Jordan to return from the men's room when I heard a phone ringing. I spotted Jordan's cell phone near his place setting and, curious, picked it up. The caller ID showed that Beverly was calling. I couldn't believe it. The two of them were on some of the same boards, but it was too late at night to be calling about business, especially on the weekend. I placed the phone back on the table and didn't mention the call to Jordan.

After dinner we strolled through the quaint little town. Its little shops and cobblestone streets reminded me of where I lived in Chestnut Hill.

"Sasha, how do you like my little hideaway?"

"It's very nice. How often do you come here in the summer?"

"I try to come every weekend, but it'll be harder this year, since I have so many more demands at the bank. Thanks to you."

"No, your thanks should go to Michael."

By the time we got back to the boat, I was exhausted from traveling all day, so I decided to go to bed early. In the small bedroom I found a hot pink eyelet teddy lying on the bed.

From behind me Jordan said, "I hope you don't mind. I thought we could have some fun tonight, 'cause it looks like this will be my last weekend on the boat."

Even though I was tired, I was also curious to see what type of fun Jordan wanted to have. "I don't mind."

He gathered my hair up and began trailing down my neck with his tongue, sending ripples of pleasure through my body.

"Why don't we start with a late-night cruise around the bay?"

"Don't you think we should wait until morning?"

Jordan headed toward the front of the boat and began to steer it into the bay. He slowly glided the boat along the moonlit water; the moment was storybook-like as I watched the shoreline lights fade away. Once we'd been moving for about forty-five minutes, he stopped the boat.

"We'll return to shore in the morning," Jordan said, then disappeared below deck. I heard a cork pop, then the soft sounds of slow music. Jordan returned with two glasses and a bottle of Cuvée Rosé Brut by Laurent-Perrier.

"This will be the most exquisite champagne you've ever tasted," Jordan promised with a soft smile.

I took two sips, savoring the light, bubbly sensation of the champagne. "You're right. This *is* exquisite."

"I'm glad you're enjoying it. I think it's the perfect champagne for toasting the good news I have for you," Jordan said, refilling my glass.

I looked at him, wondering what news he had in store. When Jordan raised his glass in a toast, I raised my glass to meet his.

Taking a deep breath, he announced, "Your man has been promoted to regional manager. And it's all because of you."

Jordan told me about his new responsibilities at the bank, making me realize how much I liked spending time with him. He was so different from Lyor, who I knew could never love me. The way I saw it, Jordan was the next best thing to Trent—he was handsome, moving up the corporate ladder, and good in bed. I just had to do something about his drinking.

I stopped Jordan from refilling his glass, then leaned back on the deck cushions and listened to the waves hitting the side of the boat. Either the wine or my desire to get away from it all made me wonder how long I could last out here without interruption from the world. I was content to remain on the deck, listening to the sea, but I could tell Jordan had other plans by the way he kept pulling me closer to him. He reached for my hand as the sounds of Marvin Gaye made their way up the stairs. At only thirty-eight years old, this man certainly loved some oldies. Following his lead, I let him take me in his arms to dance.

He spun me around. "Why don't you dance for me, Sasha?"

I laughed at his request. "You gotta be kidding."

"No, Sasha, c'mon, give me a private show."

And so I made an attempt to move to the music, but the mood and the wine were making me light-headed. Jordan appeared to enjoy seeing my body gyrate offbeat, and when I got close to him to unsnap his shorts, he decided that tonight he would take control.

He pulled down the straps of my teddy and instead of letting me step out of it, tore it off me. I was more aroused than startled by his actions.

"You ready for me?" he asked, stripping down to his jockeys. He pulled his warm yellow dick out from the opening in his shorts. Rather than enter me, he poked his hard dick around the edges of my womanhood. The anticipation of what was to come had me already about to climax, so when he suddenly thrust himself inside me, I was ready. Jordan took hold of me around my waist and brought me up to my knees, turned me over, and began to plunge in and out of me.

"Am I big enough for you now, Sasha? Uh . . . is this . . . good enough? Yeah, you didn't know I could take you like this, did you? That's right. I know how to satisfy my bitch." I was without words, so I let him have me until he pleased himself, which seemed to take forever. This was a side of Jordan I'd never seen.

The next morning my body was stiff and sticky. We'd crashed out on the deck with only a sheet to shelter us from the cool sea breeze. I threw back the sheet, but before I could get up, Jordan pushed himself back inside me and took me again. Satisfied and exhausted, I went back to sleep.

By the time I woke up, it was after noon. I jumped up,

scared that I'd missed something. Once I realized where I was, my anxieties subsided. I looked over to find Jordan naked and snoring, dick in hand. I made my way downstairs to the galley, started a pot of coffee, then showered and dressed. Standing on deck in my shorts and tank top, I noticed that we'd drifted farther away from shore than we'd been last night. Jordan began to stir, so I took him a cup of coffee, but he brushed it away and headed off to the bathroom. When he came back on deck and started the engine, he barely uttered much more than good morning to me. I could tell that he was embarrassed at the way he'd performed last night.

"What's wrong? Did I not satisfy you last night?" I asked, kissing up and down his arms as he steered the boat. I knew this couldn't be further from the truth, the way he'd yelled out my name to the ocean when he came.

"Look, I'm sorry," Jordan mumbled.

"For what?" I asked, pretending I didn't know what he meant.

"About last night."

"Why the hell do you have to be sorry? You took me the way you've been wanting to. You didn't see me trying to resist, did you?"

He turned to look at me, "Sasha, Sasha. You're too much for me. Making love with a woman like you is every man's fantasy. And you know what else?"

"What's that?"

"I think I'm falling in love with you."

Rather than go back to shore for breakfast, Jordan insisted I let him cook. He put together turkey bacon and scrambled eggs, and I lay with him on deck all day, letting him have me again and again.

We didn't return to shore until Monday morning, when I headed home. No one had heard from me since Saturday. On my drive up the highway I thought about all the things Jordan had said to me. I didn't want to be alone, but I wasn't sure if I was in love with him. Was love even necessary?

I wasn't able to think about Jordan for too long before I realized it was time to get back to business. Before I called the office, I turned on my cell phone to check my messages. There were nine. The first two were from Phoenix, and the third was from Deirdre, who had called to say that Daddy wasn't feeling well. Instead of listening to the remaining messages, I dialed Daddy's home number. The answering machine picked up. I tried both Owen and Deirdre's cell, but there was no answer there either. I couldn't think of Clara's number, so I called my office instead.

"Kendra, do you know where my father is?"

"Sasha, where have you been? Everybody's been calling here, looking for you."

"Kendra, where's my father?" I said, sharply, trying not to panic.

"I think everything is okay. I just spoke with Owen. Your father had been feeling a little dizzy, so they took him to the hospital, but I think he's all right."

"Where is my father now?"

"Owen said he's at Ms. Clara's. Do you want the number?"

"Thanks, Kendra. I'm sorry. I got caught off guard by the message that he wasn't feeling well. Anything else urgent going on?"

"Nothing urgent, but I have good news and some not-so-good news."

I tensed up before she even told me. "What's up?"

"We got the waterfront contract back, and it's been signed off on."

"Hot damn! I'll be in the office as soon as I hit Philly. Set up a dinner, a party, whatever, for the entire office. I want to take everybody out."

"And the other news is that Phoenix's gambling problem is all over the media. They're saying he's been betting on games."

"Fuck! Make me a reservation to fly to Chicago, and I'm going to need you and Tiffany to go with me. I'll call you back."

Before I could dial Phoenix's number, my cell phone rang. It was Owen.

"Owen, what happened to Daddy?"

"He's okay, Ma. He got a little dizzy and nauseous last night, so we took him to the emergency room. They wound up lowering the dosage on his medication."

"Where's Daddy at now?"

"He's over Ms. Clara's. I just called there, and he's sleeping. Ma, are you all right?"

"Yes, I'm fine. I'm sorry you couldn't reach me. I was out on that damn boat with Jordan and couldn't get any service."

"I guess you heard your boy Phoenix is all over the news."

I didn't even have a chance to answer him before my line beeped again.

"Owen, I gotta go, that's Phoenix on the other line."

"Yes, Ma. I'll see you when you get back home."

"Sasha, where the fuck have you been? Shit is outta control! Just like I told you, that bastard waited until the season started. Now all this shit is in the news."

"Phoenix, what happened?"

"What happened? Where the fuck are you, in outer fucking space? They are saying that I shaved points during last year's play-off games."

"I'll be in Chicago in a few hours. I'm going to schedule a press conference for this week. Until then, don't say a thing to the media or anybody else—you hear me? What's the commissioner saying?"

"Don't you understand? They're coming up here this afternoon to meet with me and Mitchell."

"What's Mitchell saying?"

"My sponsors are calling Mitchell, wanting to know what the hell is going on."

"Phoenix?"

"What?"

"What's the status on the diamonds?"

"Nothing. I'm not making any moves. They can have that shit, it's not worth my fuckin' career."

"Phoenix, who the hell is this guy?"

"Brit Kostas—he's only a fall guy for LT, I fuckin' know it. Look, I have to go into a team meeting. I'll see you when you get here. Hurry the fuck up."

After I hung up with Phoenix, my phone rang again.

"Sasha, it's me—just wanted to remind you not to forget about Arshell and Wayne's anniversary party arrangements. And Harry Bowen just called—he wants to speak to you about coming to California after the holidays," Kendra said, reminding me that I had a full workload.

"What about the flights? Did you find out anything?"

"The latest flight to Chicago is at eight tonight. Do you think you can make it by then?"

"No, I have to see Daddy before I go anywhere. See how early I can leave in the morning."

Just when I thought I couldn't take another phone call, message, or problem, I got that old familiar feeling. I prayed it wasn't really happening while I was driving. I tried to ignore the pounding in my chest, and the light-headedness that made me feel as if my head were sliding down my neck. Not only was my world spinning out of control, but my body was giving out on me, too. How could all this happen in one weekend? I slowly reached over and turned off my cell phone and the radio, while trying to keep my eyes on the road.

I was scared to pull over; if I did, I might never get home. I had to hold on. Even though none of these feelings were foreign, it had still been a while since I'd had them. This had to be the worst episode yet.

I talked to myself as I nervously drove over the Bay Bridge. I turned the static-filled radio back on so I wouldn't be so consumed by my thoughts. I thought about the porn videos lying under my bed—my remedy for these attacks. Too bad I didn't have a television in the Range's dashboard. Then I laughed. There was no way I could watch that shit and drive.

Michael had unknowingly turned me on to those damn movies. About two years ago he'd invited me to his birthday party, and before leaving the office, which at the time was still in my house, I'd found a package on his desk with a yellow sticky marked "Return to Shelly." I'd assumed Michael had forgotten to take it with him, so I put it in my briefcase so I could give it to him at the party. Once I got there, I forgot all about it.

When I got home that night, I was a little restless and decided to pop the tape in my VCR. It looked a little interesting from the title, *Sistas Loving Sistas.* However, these sistas were doing more than just loving each other.

I watched, wondering what it would feel like to take on a different identity and be one of these women. I laughed at the noises they made, and wondered if I made those same sounds or if my face held those same expressions when I was in my moments of ecstasy. I thought the video was funny until I felt myself getting aroused. Rather than watch it all the way through, I turned it off. Then one Sunday afternoon, while I lay in bed in the midst of an anxiety attack, rather than take Paxil, I turned on the television, forgetting that the tape was still in the DVD.

This time I didn't find the video funny or disgusting. These women's passion didn't seem dirty or contrived. I allowed myself to watch as they discovered each other's bodies, massaging each other's breasts, stomachs, and thighs, always trying something creative to make the moment last. Watching not only calmed my racing heart that Sunday afternoon, it aroused me, and before I knew it, I was using my own hands to satisfy myself.

13

BURNT OFFERINGS

After getting into Philly last night, I'd gone directly to see Daddy, who was staying at Clara's. Then I met Kendra and Tiffany at the office, where we prepared for Phoenix's press conference, and I talked to Mitchell in between. I was exhausted.

Tiffany, Kendra, and I flew into Chicago at seven o'clock in the morning. We all agreed that Phoenix was about to take a big hit. His meeting with the commissioner had been short. We learned that the NBA would do a complete investigation of the allegations made by Brit Kostas, a well-known rich but sleazy gambler, to find out if a criminal act had been committed. Mitchell was already putting together evidence to weaken Kostas's credibility, which Phoenix said wouldn't be hard to do.

Rather than check into the hotel, we went straight to

Carter Enterprises. The press conference was scheduled for noon the next afternoon at the arena. Until the allegations had been confirmed, Phoenix had the full support of his teammates and head office. I'd asked all of them to be present for the press conference; some of them, I'm sure, didn't have a choice.

Later that night Phoenix came to my room to strategize for the press conference. We hoped the press didn't know all the dirty details.

When Phoenix entered my room, he was drained from two practices, dodging the media, and trying to come to grips with the fact that his career was on thin ice. Even Crystal was threatening to leave him once all this was over. Phoenix grew angry as we watched late-night talk shows make fun of his dilemma.

"I got a fucking bull's-eye on my back."

"What's the worst case scenario from the commissioner?"

"If they find out I've been point shaving, I'll have to retire, and then the Feds will pick it up."

"You know your apparel sales are skyrocketing."

"Mitchell told me. Sasha, the fucking media has dissected my entire life in the paper."

He sat there with his head in his hands, and I felt I had to go to him. I rubbed the back of his bald head. He placed his arms around my waist and held on to me.

"What do you think? You think we can turn this around?"

I knelt down in front of him. "Remember, I'm Sasha Borianni, and you're Phoenix Carter. We built our careers off each other, and I'm not going to let you go down. When you retire, it'll be your choice."

Then it happened, really easy, as if it were supposed to. I cradled his head in my hands, bringing his lips to mine. I refused to think about the consequences.

"Oh, shit, Sasha, I need you so bad," he said through kisses that took my breath away.

"And tonight you can have me—c'mon, lay back."

He lay on the bed, and I stretched my body onto his, taking his shirt out of his pants, unbuckling his belt. Rather than unbutton it, he pulled my blouse apart and turned me over, his body on top of mine, his lips barely leaving mine. "Oh, God, I love you. I swear I'm not letting you go this time." Before I could utter the words "I love you" back, there was a knock on the door.

He took his mouth from mine. "Who is it?" he asked, pissed at the interruption.

"It's Trey. Man, you gotta get outta here."

At that moment we knew Trey had saved us from venturing onto dangerous ground.

"It's all right, just go. I'll see you later," I told him as Trey knocked again, this time harder.

"Phoenix, man, come the fuck on, the paparazzi are all over this joint."

"Sasha, I can't leave you like this. They can wait."

"No, you should go. Listen to Trey."

Once Phoenix was gone, I called Jordan—I needed someone to pull me out of Phoenix's grip. We didn't talk long because he sounded distracted, complaining that he had a breakfast meeting. I phoned Arshell, but she was asleep. The only other person I wanted to talk to was Trent.

"This is a surprise," he said. "I thought you'd forgotten about me."

"I've just been busy."

"I can see by watching the news. You have your hands full."

"I know."

"You don't sound good. Is everything okay?"

"I'm fine, just sitting up here in a lonely hotel room." I knew that was probably the wrong thing to say, but I couldn't help myself.

"You need some company?"

"Trent, I need more than you can imagine. Maybe we can go to dinner or something when I get back."

"That works for me."

In the morning I phoned Lyor and left him a message, telling him where I was. As soon as I hung up, he called me back.

"Sasha, what's going on? Are you surviving up there? Don't worry about the Panache board meeting, I rescheduled it until after you return."

"Thanks, Lyor. I really appreciate that."

"How are you holding up with all this stuff with Phoenix?"

"It doesn't look good. Every time you think it's wrapped up, there's another twist. It's very draining."

"I know you don't like to discuss your clients, but you know I'm here if you need to sort some of this out."

"Will I see you when I get home?"

"That's not even a question."

After speaking with Lyor, I got dressed and headed for the arena.

Standing in the conference room at the Chicago Center, I was amazed at the number of reporters. In all my years doing public relations I'd never seen anything like it, except when the president held a press conference.

When Phoenix and Crystal stepped into the room, I braced myself. He appeared calm and confident, as if he was there for an after-game press conference, but we both knew this was a serious matter. He spoke crisply and clearly.

"Thank you for coming today. You've all heard about the allegations that have been made against me, and more importantly, my character. These rumors have been created maliciously to blemish my basketball career. I will not allow that to happen. I am confident that after the NBA completes its investigation, they will find that at no time did I ever violate league rules."

After his short statement, Phoenix left the room. I knew there was nothing more I could do for him, except stand by his side and hope the NBA did not find hard evidence about his gambling and point shaving. Leaving the arena, I decided to turn my attention back to my own life, particularly my sick father and my adulterous best friend.

14

PENDULUM

Even though Arshell and Wayne were having marital problems and she'd chosen to deal with them by taking a lover, Wayne was being the ever-faithful husband. He asked me to help him plan a twentieth-wedding anniversary party for them, which would be a surprise to Arshell. I couldn't believe Arshell was still cheating on Wayne. She always seemed preoccupied—even toward me—so I knew Wayne was doing all this to please her. In the last year they'd gone from a three-bedroom townhouse to a single-family home in Hampshire Greens Estates in Aston, Maryland. Arshell was messing with a good thing.

I'd enlisted Kendra's help to plan the party. We'd decided to hold the event at the Glenview Mansion in Rockville, Maryland. To get Arshell to the party, Wayne would tell her he was taking her there for a romantic dinner.

Two days before the party Kendra had gone down to Maryland to ensure everything would go as planned. Jordan and I drove down in my Range Rover the morning of the party. While Jordan drove, I turned the front seat into a makeshift office, making calls and responding to e-mails.

"Can't you give work a break?" he asked.

"I'm sorry."

"Yeah, well, I wanted to talk to you about some things."

I could tell he was serious, so I closed my Blackberry and put my phone on vibrate. This wasn't a time for me to be unavailable, especially to Phoenix, who'd grown dependent on talking to me at least twice a day.

"What's so serious, Jordan?"

"It's not that it's serious, but I need to talk to you—is that okay?"

Something was definitely on his mind. "Sure."

"I'm thinking about moving out of the city, you know, to the suburbs, and I was hoping you'd want to help me look for a house."

"Jordan, that's great. Where do you want to go?"

"What do you think about Lower Merion? I've heard you can get a nice house out there for about three hundred."

"Sure, I'll help you. Have you hired a realtor yet?"

"That's all taken care of, but I need you to look at some houses with the realtor."

"Of course I'll go," I said, not knowing where I'd get the time.

"Good, but that's not all. Sasha, I don't want you to answer me now, I just want you to think about what I'm going to say."

What the hell was he going to ask me?

"I know we've never talked about it before, and I know you're older and probably done with this, but would you think about . . . consider having another child?"

A burst of laughter came out before I could even respond. "Jordan, you can't be serious."

"This is no joke, Sasha. If I'm going to consider marrying you, then I need to know if you'd be willing to have my children. Like I said, I don't want you to answer me now."

Good thing he didn't, because I couldn't answer him. In all the months that we'd been seeing each other, I never thought he'd ask me that. His career was on the fast track, as was mine. I thought that eventually we'd get married, and I would've even been willing to move to the suburbs. But a child, hell no.

Shortly after that bombshell, we checked into a suite at the Doubletree Hotel in Rockville, where Kendra had reserved a block of rooms. I'd been hoping to stay an extra night with Jordan, but I couldn't even think of that now.

Jordan's mood had soured our conversation, and I wasn't sure how to approach him. Then I remembered the wine, which he always used to relax. I was sure he'd packed a bottle, so while he was out buying shaving cream, I poured him a glass of wine and prepared to take a shower to be ready for him when he returned. I was standing naked in the bathroom when he suddenly reappeared.

"Sasha, what are you doing here?" he asked. "Drinking alone? You know that's a sign of an alcoholic."

"I thought you were going to the store," I said, noticing he didn't have a bag.

"I'm surprised to see you're not on the phone."

There was an edge in his voice, but now I knew how to get rid of it. I turned around and moved close to him, close enough to start pulling down the zipper of his pants.

"Hey, what are you doing?"

"I thought we could relax before the party."

"Oh, no, working lady. You better call the office, check your messages, make sure your clients don't need you."

I knelt in front of him. "Shut up, Jordan."

"Sasha, you know we don't have time for this."

I looked up at him, his dick in my hand, "Jordan, shut up."

When I saw him grab the side of the doorway, I knew I had his attention. I opened my mouth wide and brought him inside my mouth until the tip of his dick tickled the back of my throat. I heard him grunt. I pulled him back out, and this time, even slower, I took him in again and let his dick lie on my tongue until he moaned. I knew I had him, weakened, with no thoughts of children. "Sasha, wait, hold it. Let me sit down."

There was no waiting. His dick was hard enough that I didn't even have to hold it steady with my hands. He grabbed his dick and pushed it in and out of my mouth until I tasted droplets of cum. He was on his way to where I wanted to take him.

Jordan picked up the glass of wine and literally poured it between my mouth and his dick. But that didn't stop me. I licked his dick, his balls, and everywhere I tasted cum.

To keep him from falling, I pushed him back toward the bed. He sat on the edge of bed, allowing me to lick and tease the head of his dick with my tongue.

"Sash . . . a, oh, oh, oh." And with those words I knew he was done. With Jordan sprawled on the bed, I showered and dressed, then woke him.

It was a good thing the mansion was only about five minutes away, because we were running late.

While Jordan sped along Rockville Pike, I scanned the guest list that Kendra had left at the hotel for me. My eyes locked in on a name I should've expected to see: Trent L. Russell.

"Damn it!" I said loudly.

"Is everything all right?" Jordan asked, turning to look at me.

"Yes, I just saw a name that I didn't expect. I mean I did, I just didn't think."

"Is there going to be a problem?"

"No, not really."

Since talking to Trent in Chicago, I'd kept wavering on talking to or seeing him again. I wasn't sure if it was the smart thing to do. I had been stupid not to think he'd be at Wayne and Arshell's party. He was their friend, too.

Glenview was a nineteenth-century mansion spread out over one hundred and fifty acres. Stepping into the grand lobby, with its marbled floors and ornate chandeliers, I felt like I'd stepped back in time. I heard Jordan whisper behind me, "This would be a great place to get married."

Kendra met us at the entrance to the conservatory where the party was being held. Since the room hadn't filled up yet, it was easy to see that Trent hadn't yet arrived. An hour later the room had filled up, and when Wayne and Arshell arrived, Arshell appeared to be genuinely surprised.

I watched Arshell mingle with her friends and Wayne's coworkers. Either she was a good actress or she was really enjoying herself. Every chance she got, she kept telling me that we had to talk. I could tell it was something I didn't want to hear.

I had yet to see Trent. Maybe he'd changed his mind about coming. I excused myself after dancing with Jordan and headed for the ladies' room.

I stopped in my tracks when I saw Trent dancing with Arshell. I watched his body move as he spun her around in circles, laughing. I missed him. When the music changed to a slow song, Trent walked across the room to stand beside a woman who I guessed was his date.

While I was trying to decide whether to approach him and say hello, Arshell came up and swished me away to another room. I wanted to ask her about the woman Trent was with, but she was too excited about whatever it was she had to tell me.

"You're not going to believe what I did," she said, moving around excitedly.

"What, go see a doctor like I suggested?"

She moved closer and whispered, "No, no, this is something better. I want you to guess."

I rolled my eyes. "I don't know. What, had some wild and crazy sex? Wait, maybe you broke it off with him?"

"Sasha, c'mon, don't say that."

"All right, go 'head. Tell me."

"Okay, he's been asking me about my fantasies, and even though I'd hinted around about what they really were, I never thought he'd actually try to make them come true."

Now I was worried. I knew all too well how dangerous fantasies could be. "Arshell, what did you do?"

"You're going to be jealous, 'cause I don't think you've ever done it. At least you've never told me. I've already promised myself I'll never do it again, but it was soooo good."

"Please, Arshell." I prayed she wasn't going to tell me she'd taken some damn drugs.

"We did it. The three of us."

"You did *what!*" I screamed. She quickly covered my mouth with her hand.

Yanking her by the arm, I pulled her over to the window, out of earshot of anybody passing by.

"Arshell, are you outta your fucking mind? What the hell is wrong with you? You're married. You can't be doing that shit."

"Why not?" she asked, her face filled with disappointment that I wasn't willing to share in her new experience.

"Arshell, I don't want to talk about this. Especially right now. Your husband is throwing this great party for you, and you want to tell me about a damn threesome you had with a man and some strange woman!"

"That's what I'm trying to tell you, it wasn't another woman. I was with my mechanic and one of his friends."

"My God, Arshell, you don't know these men. You could've been hurt. I can't believe you were that stupid."

She backed away from me. "So I see, that's how it is. Now that you have your little banker boyfriend, you think you're better than me. Well, you need to remember it wasn't too long ago that your ass was running around fucking everybody. I guess you don't see Trent in there. The man you missed out on marrying. Remember, I was the one who supported your ass through all that shit."

Her words cut deep, but I refused to let up. "Does

that mean I'm supposed to sit here and ask you how it was? Ask you whose dick went where? Arshell, you gotta get a grip."

"Well, don't expect me to sit around listening when you start fucking Phoenix Carter again."

"You're the one that has the husband and kids."

"Everything you wanted but never had, right?"

I couldn't take any more. I walked away.

She screamed after me, "Sasha, wait! Please, I'm sorry."

I was ready to leave, but before I could find Jordan in the crowded and loud ballroom, I found myself face to face with Trent and his date. He ignored my obvious frustration and introduced us.

"Veronica, this is Sasha. Sasha, Veronica."

"Hello, Veronica, I'm glad you could make it."

I detested her. She was petite and gorgeous with a flattering shape. She obviously had good taste—she was with Trent, *and* she was dressed in an elegant pink chiffon skirt and black jacket.

We shook hands.

"Sasha, I've been reading about your firm, Platinum—"

"Images," I said, cutting off her search for the full name of my firm.

"We're so looking forward to having you work on Trent's campaign."

I had no idea what she was talking about and gave Trent a look that said so.

"Yes, Sasha and I have an appointment to iron out the details."

"Can the two of you please excuse me?" Veronica asked, then stepped around me and headed for the ladies' room.

When she walked away, I asked, "Trent, what the hell is she talking about?"

"I'd mentioned to her that I'd met you for breakfast, and she immediately assumed that it was about the campaign."

"But I told you I wasn't working with you."

"And I don't expect you to. Let's just forget about Veronica, okay?"

I took a deep breath, "All right, let's start over."

He kissed me on the cheek. "You look awesome tonight. I saw your date over there at the bar," he said, pointing to Jordan, who was in deep conversation with Wayne.

"He's more than that, Trent, we're planning to get married."

"Why are you always fighting with me? Am I that bad?"

Before answering, I took the time to really look at him. He was dressed in a tailored black one-button, single-breasted suit and white shirt.

"You never dressed like that when we dated."

"Veronica dresses me. I told you, she's a buyer at Barney's."

"Yes, I remember."

"You've let your beard grow in," I said, taking in the scent of his Mont Blanc cologne. It smelled nowhere near the same on Jordan.

"You like it?" he asked, touching his face with his hands. "Sasha, I'm not going to make this easy on you."

"You're wasting your time," I said, spotting Veronica as she made her way to us. "It was nice meeting you, Veronica, but if you'll both excuse me, I'm in search of my date.

"Jordan, I'm ready to go. I'm tired."

"Are you tired, or do you want to have some fun tonight?"

"No, just tired."

After Arshell's news and seeing Trent with his woman, sex was the last thing I was wanted.

Back at the hotel I had to deal with an oversexed, drunk Jordan. While I undressed, Jordan pawed all over me. But instead of feeling good, I felt dirty. I realized I didn't really love Jordan. I just loved the idea of us being together, a "power couple." Climbing on top of him, I was forced to breathe in his alcohol-tainted breath. I let my imagination take over and replaced Jordan with Phoenix, Trent, even Lyor.

15

MYTHS

I was glad to be back to work. I needed some time away from Jordan and his talk of marriage and children. By midweek he'd already had a realtor contact me about listings, but I had no idea where I was going to get the time to look at houses. The one thing that I didn't have to worry about at the moment was Phoenix. Basketball season had begun, and even though the papers still reported rumors of his point shaving, the NBA had privately agreed to ease off its investigation until the end of the season. Brit Kostas had yet to speak to the newspapers, which was in our favor. Luckily, all the talk of the allegations against Phoenix had every arena sold out, which was making the NBA happy. Phoenix's fans were behind him and showed that support by boosting his apparel sales.

Between dealing with Phoenix, lusting after Trent,

and trying to keep Arshell from ruining her marriage, I was finally able to celebrate the Harry Bowen deal. Platinum Images would be handling the publicity for Bowen Entertainment's films for one year. It would also be our job to ensure that the relationship between Bowen Entertainment and the Philadelphia community was positive, as filming can often be disruptive to the community in which it takes place.

I made reservations at a Caribbean soul-food restaurant called Bluezette for myself, Kendra, Michael, and Tiffany. When we arrived, we ordered drinks at the bar. By the time we were seated, we'd already downed one bottle of champagne. The waitress brought our menus and told us about the specials as we perused the entrée selections.

"What is all this shit? I don't know what to order," Kendra complained, not even wanting to try to figure out the menu. "I thought this was a soul-food restaurant."

"Upscale Caribbean soul food, sweetheart," Tiffany said.

"I'll tell you this, the one thing I do know how to select is a good bottle of wine," I said, ordering a carafe of Junmai Daiginjo.

"That's right, I forgot—you have a wino for a boyfriend," Michael muttered.

"Very funny, Michael. I'll have you know Jordan Ashe is a wine connoisseur."

"Looks to me like his nose is wide open for you," Tiffany said, without looking up from her drink.

"And he isn't the only one," Kendra whispered into her menu.

"And just who might you be talking about?"

"The big gun, Mr. Phoenix 'Rising' Carter. Isn't he the one who gets all your attention?"

"You're right, Kendra. I don't think she's looked at any other projects since he came on board," Tiffany added.

"Okay, but just remember that big gun is paying some big bucks," I retorted. Tiffany gestured toward Michael and said, "Wait a minute, is it possible that you don't have a blazer on tonight?"

"I only wear blazers to work. But if I did want to wear one, sweetie, I could select from thirty. More, I'm sure, than your closet full of short skirts."

"That's how Tiffany gets her clients, isn't it?" Kendra joked.

It was Michael's turn. "Kendra, I know you're not talking, 'cause you're the one that comes in to work every day with a different hair color to match your outfit."

"Aw, c'mon, y'all. It's not every day, just twice a week."

"Whatever," Michael added.

In stitches, I gestured to Kendra and Tiffany to observe how Michael ate his food.

After watching him for a moment, I asked, "Michael, does eating one thing at a time prolong your meal?"

"Oh, I see. You have jokes. If you need to know, it actually helps me to enjoy the flavor of each item."

Kendra, Tiffany, and I laughed.

Looking at the three of them, I prayed that I'd forever have them as a part of my life and business.

Later that week, on my way home from the office I received an excited call from Lyor, practically begging me to attend a Flyers game with him. I tried to tell him that I don't do hockey, but he convinced me to go by offering to get me floor seats to the next Sixers home game. How could I possibly say no to a man who begged? Especially since I knew I would give the tickets to Owen.

I turned around and drove back down Lincoln Drive and over the expressway to meet him at the Wachovia Center. Once I picked up my ticket from the will-call window, I joined Lyor at our seats outside the penalty box. The place was freezing cold but Lyor insisted that we drink beer to get into the mood. Lyor explained the game, because I simply couldn't understand why the players changed so frequently. All I could really figure out was that the goalie was the one who actually controlled the game by not letting the puck get past him.

The stadium was filled with white people, men and young boys mostly. I pointed out to Lyor that I was probably one of ten black people present, and the only black woman. Suddenly the crowd went wild as the players started fighting. Unlike in other sports, fighting is allowed in hockey—encouraged almost—which is probably the reason why most of the players don't have their own teeth. Lyor's excitement at watching the game was infectious. I began to enjoy the gracefulness of the skating mixed with the roughness of the sport.

After the game I suggested that Lyor follow me back to my house for a nightcap. I was quite horny from watching the game, and I needed to pee to get rid of all that beer. It was the first time Lyor had been to my place, and I told him to make himself comfortable. Sitting on the toilet for what seemed like a full ten minutes, I began to imagine being with a white man. I conjured up all the myths and jokes I'd heard over the years, one of which he'd already proven to be true by the way he'd gone down on me in Miami.

Back downstairs, I joined Lyor on the couch, where he was watching CNN. The newscaster was droning on about the stock market, and not until I felt him kissing me did I realize I'd dozed off.

"I'm sorry, did I fall asleep?"

"That's how I like you, quiet, relaxed."

"You know how I like you?"

"How's that?"

"Take me upstairs, and I'll remind you. I should take a shower," I said, trying to delay, knowing I was already moist in anticipation.

"No, please don't. This is just how I want you, spicy."

"But, Lyor . . ."

"Shhh. Quiet, relaxed."

I nodded my head yes, because he'd already begun to pull my sweater over my head. Reaching behind me, he unhooked my bra, letting my breasts fill his waiting hands. He was right; this couldn't have waited. He buried his face between them until my arousal caused me to squirm on the couch. He stood up, removed his clothes, and came back to me. When I tried to stand up and take off my jeans, he insisted on doing it for me.

With both of us fully naked, he just stared at me without touching, like he couldn't believe what he was seeing.

He licked his thin lips. "Come to me, Sasha," he said, sitting back down on the couch.

I knew what he wanted.

I positioned myself between his thighs, where I reached down and caressed the heaviness that hung between his legs. The size thing had also been a myth.

"You would like to have that?" he asked.

I straddled him and rubbed the tip of his penis against my wetness. When I couldn't take any more of his teasing, I began to ease myself down on him. But he pulled back.

"Lie down. I want to try something," he said, urging me onto my back.

I didn't want to try anything—I wanted him inside me right now. But I waited. He was looking around the room. For what, I didn't know. Finally he picked up my bra from where it lay on the floor and placed it over my eyes, blindfolding me.

I waited for him to do something, but I could only feel his fingers tracing the outline of my body. It was strange not knowing from which direction he was going to take me. And then he had his way. He inserted his tongue as far as it would go deep inside me, then stopped. I grabbed for him, but he wasn't within reach.

"Lyor, please."

He answered my pleas by dipping his finger into the sticky wetness between my legs, then rubbing that same finger against my lips, making me taste myself. He was so good at this, at making my body talk to him. I let my inhibitions go. Again I tried to grab for him, and I found him buried between my legs. Raising my legs above his head, he went in and out of my wetness, licking me and sucking me from one hole to the other and everywhere in between. Lyor was sucking the life out of me. He was truly a master at this game. Just when I felt he'd exhausted all my strength, I reached my orgasm. But he wasn't finished. He flipped me over, pulled me up on my knees, and rode me into submission.

I had no idea what time it was when I heard him say, "Sasha, I have to go." What I did know was that I was back in a game I thought I'd graduated from.

16

HAPPY BIRTHDAY

November

Birthdays had always been a good time for me when I was growing up. Even as I'd gotten older, I still enjoyed the celebration, and this year, the office staff surprised me with a cake, balloons, flowers, and some really nice gifts.

Later that evening Jordan accompanied me to Daddy's for dinner. It somewhat bothered me that I didn't feel guilty about having slept with Lyor. I attributed it to my old habits trying to nestle their way back into my life. I knew I couldn't allow myself to be caught up between two men again. But I tried to tell myself they were two separate entities, that one had nothing to do with the other.

Clara's cooking that night was outstanding, and I

could see why Daddy loved her. She'd made hot fried chicken, cabbage, mashed potatoes, gravy, and cornbread. I loved her, too.

My grandchildren were excited regardless of whose birthday it was and loaded up on a homemade butter cake that I'd watched Jordan make the night before. I felt like a little girl again with all the attention and gifts I'd received. Daddy gave me his usual card with $100, but this time he'd surprised me by presenting me with a scrapbook that went from my childhood to the open house of Platinum Images.

Deirdre and Owen gave me a beautiful silver Tiffany watch, and the grandchildren each gave me all kinds of things they'd made. But Jordan's gift, though striking, was somewhat disappointing. He gave me a custom-framed rOMAN gABRIEL photograph. I'm sure it had cost him a lot of money, but I'd been looking for something more personal. I'd been hoping that for my birthday we'd make a further commitment, an engagement. I needed it as a shield from further thoughts of sexual liaisons with Lyor.

On the way back to my house, all Jordan could talk about was the cable television account he'd just landed. He apologized for not having been around a lot lately and offered to take me on vacation with him after the holidays.

My real disappointment came after we'd had a champagne toast and I was ready to settle in with him for the night. He told me that me he couldn't stay over, that he had a meeting early the next morning.

With him gone, I phoned Arshell.

"Happy Birthday, girl. I left you a message on your cell phone."

"Thanks, I got it. I'm so sorry for letting what happened between us at your party keep me from calling you."

"Sasha, I'm the one that needs to apologize. I'm sorry too. I shouldn't have expected you to go along with whatever crazy shit I'm doing."

"You're still doing him?"

"And well."

"When do I get to hear the details about this threesome you had?"

"Really?"

"Yep, give up the scoop."

We sat there on the phone for two hours while she told me all about her mechanic and her threesome. There was no denying that this man really turned her on. But Arshell remained committed to her family.

Just as I was hanging up with Arshell, the line beeped. When I answered the waiting call, someone sang "Happy Birthday" to me.

"Trent?"

"Hey, birthday girl."

"That was so nice, but I told you a long time ago that you couldn't hold a note."

"But you never stopped me from singing to you."

"I just didn't want to hurt your feelings."

"Sasha, what are you doing home on your birthday? You're supposed to be out celebrating with that man of yours."

"I did. We had dinner at Daddy's."

"And you're home by yourself?"

"Trent, don't go there."

"You sure? Because I could drive down there right now and take you out on the town."

"You're a crazy man. Anyway, I gotta go. I have an early-morning conference call I have to prepare for."

"So that means we don't get to hang out?"

"Good night, Trent."

For the rest of the night, for my birthday, I sat in bed watching CNN.

At work the next day things started looking up when a large box from a furrier in Chicago arrived. With Michael, Kendra, and Tiffany standing close by in anticipation, I opened it, knowing it was from Phoenix. Inside was the most beautiful coat I'd ever seen.

"Chinchilla," Kendra said before I could even get it all the way out the garment bag.

"Damn, that brother must really appreciate you," Tiffany said, rubbing her hands on the coat.

"We go a long way back," I responded, slipping my arms into the sleeves of the coat. "I guess this means I'll be spending a lot of time in Chicago."

"Here, let me have it. I'll go," Kendra offered.

In the midst of Tiffany and Kendra taking turns strutting around the office in the chinchilla, Lyor phoned.

"Happy Birthday, my cornflakes brown sista. Sounds like you guys are having a party."

"Thank you, Lyor. Where are you?"

"I have a present for you."

"Really? And when am I going to get it, if you're still out of town?"

"Can you be at my house tonight at seven o'clock sharp?"

"But I thought you weren't coming back from Chicago until tomorrow."

"One thing has nothing to do with the other. By the way, how is your father doing?"

"Better. Lyor, how am I supposed to get in?"

"You will find a key in your top desk drawer." While listening to him, I pulled open my top drawer. There I found a single key.

"Hey, how'd you get that in there?"

"Ahh, your receptionist likes me."

"Why so sneaky?"

"Birthday presents are meant to be a surprise. Will you be there?"

"Lyor, are you coming back tonight?"

"Just be there at seven to receive your present. Goodbye, Sasha."

All day I wondered what he could be getting me. I asked Tiffany if she knew anything about this mysterious birthday present, but she gave me her usual attitude when it came to him.

"Tiff, listen. I'm leaving to go to Lyor's. He didn't happen to say anything to you about a birthday present?"

"No, I haven't spoken to him. He's away, right? Why? What did he get you?"

"I don't know. I'll find out when I get to his place."

"Just be careful with him."

"You're always telling me that."

"It's not that I don't like him. I just don't trust him."

"You're just saying that because he's white."

"Well, maybe. But only time will tell."

I reached the Victor that evening fifteen minutes early. Using my key, I entered the candlelit condo. Soft music floated from the suite's speakers.

"Lyor?" I called out from where I stood in the open doorway.

In response, out of the bedroom walked a woman who looked to be Dominican by the color of her skin. I assumed she was serving Lyor and me dinner, judging by her uniform: a black zip-up T-shirt and short black skirt.

Bowing her head in introduction, she greeted me, "Hello, Ms. Borianni. I'm Senta."

"Hello, Senta. Where's Lyor?"

"You look surprised to see me."

Closing the door, I answered, "Well, I am."

"I'm sorry. Mr. Lyor didn't tell you that I'd be your masseuse tonight?"

I smiled, relieved. Lyor was so good sometimes. I'd been complaining lately about being stressed and how I'd love to take the time to go to Spa Bavu for a massage.

"Senta, I couldn't be more pleased. What do you need me to do?" I said, hastily removing my coat.

"All you need to do is get undressed and step into the bathroom, where I've drawn you a warm bath."

In Lyor's bathroom the scent of magnolias filled the air. The bathtub was filled with bubbles, and the entire room was illuminated by candlelight. I quickly undressed, threw my clothes across a chair in Lyor's room, and was stepping into the bathwater when Senta appeared in the doorway.

"Is the water temperature okay?"

"It's perfect." I stretched out, allowing the warmth and silkiness of the water to move around me. I watched Senta gather her oils and towels and take them into the other room. She was an attractive woman, probably about twenty-five, with auburn hair pulled back in a bun and breasts that pushed out above the zipper of her shirt. I wondered if she was Lyor's personal masseuse.

"Ms. Borianni, would you like me to sponge you off?"

"That would be nice."

She kneeled down on a folded towel and used a scented

loofah to squeeze warm water onto my neck, back, and breasts. I closed my eyes and imagined being under a waterfall. She lathered my body and rinsed me off as if I were a baby, and just when I felt I could have nodded off to sleep, she held out a large white towel.

"Thank you, Senta," I said, feeling good that I didn't even have to dry my own body. Lyor really knew how to make me feel special.

Guiding me into Lyor's bedroom, she said, "Whenever you're ready, you can lie down."

I stretched out across Lyor's white Egyptian cotton sheets.

"Senta, are you sure that Lyor isn't coming home?"

"I don't know, Ms. Borianni. He just phoned our salon and chose the relaxing Swedish massage for you."

Once I was comfortable, Senta covered me with a sheet and began to gently touch me through the sheet to warm my body. Then she uncovered my shoulders and arms. With her soft, oiled hands she applied just the right amount of pressure to untangle the knots that had made themselves part of my body. Moving down to my back, she worked my muscles until I let out an embarrassing moan.

"It's okay, Ms. Borianni. It's your birthday."

Yes, I deserved everything I received except that damn piece of art Jordan had given me. I didn't understand why there had been no night out, no weekend getaway. Caught up in thoughts of Jordan, I didn't notice Senta kneading the cheeks of my ass.

She must've sensed that I needed to be taken out of my own thoughts. "Relax, it's okay," Senta said, covering my upper body. She now focused on my legs, giving me long strokes up and down my thighs, using her hands, even her forearms. I thought I heard her whisper, "You have beautiful legs."

"You can turn over now," she said, this time louder.

I turned over, giving her the front of me. She began with my shoulders, and then with her fingertips she lightly massaged my breasts. My nipples hardened in response. She tried to relax them by circling them with the palms of her hands, but it only made it worse.

Senta moved down to massage the front of my legs, and when she reached my inner thighs, I was positive she could see the pulse beating in my womanhood and I hoped she would massage that, too. She moved farther down my body to my feet and massaged spots there that had me almost to the point of ecstasy.

"Does it feel all right, Ms. Borianni?"

I wanted to tell her to do whatever it is a woman does to make love to another woman, but I couldn't get the words out. I must've watched too many of those tapes.

Just when my body began to melt into the bed, I felt Senta's hands move between my thighs, stroking the warm wetness that had gathered between my legs. I gripped the sheet, hoping to pull myself out of this trance, but I was in too deep.

In Spanish, Senta whispered words that I couldn't understand as she brought a hard rush of orgasm through my body. When it was over, I heard her asking me if I was okay, but my response was only a low murmur of satisfaction.

When I woke up it felt like hours later. I sensed movement in the room, and I thought it was Lyor's cat, Cashmere. But when I opened my eyes, it was Lyor, standing there watching me sleep.

"Happy Birthday," he said, nodding toward the pillow next to me. I smiled weakly back at him. Beside me on the pillow lay a black box with a silver bow. He sat next to me on the bed and handed me the box. I removed the bow and its ribbon, pulled off the cover, and was shocked and practically blinded by the most beautiful diamond necklace I'd ever seen. It appeared to be held together by nothing at all.

"The eternity necklace," he said, lifting it from the cushion where it lay.

I felt my eyes water. "Lyor, why'd you do this? I can't—"

"You cannot what, Sasha? You didn't think that a mere massage was all I was going to give to you?"

And that's when I remembered why I was in his bed, naked. Noticing the embarrassed look on my face, he said, "How was your massage? Did you enjoy Senta?"

"She was very nice. But Lyor, I should tell you—"

"Shhh, do not tell me anything. Here, sit up. Let me put this on you."

He placed the eternity necklace on my neck and held up a mirror for me to see. The word thank-you didn't seem to be enough to convey my appreciation.

"I love you, Lyor."

"I love you, too. Now go back to sleep."

17

HAPPY HOLIDAYS

As the holidays began to roll in, things at work quieted down. There was still no word from the NBA on their investigation of Phoenix, and even the press laid off for a while. We still spoke daily, but neither of us mentioned what had almost happened in my Chicago hotel room. I'd spent Thanksgiving with my family, and now that it was Christmas, the office would be closed for two weeks. I'd joined a Pilates class at a local spa, and when I wasn't at Daddy's, I was at home working. Arshell and her mechanic were still going strong, and she seemed happier with her home life. I guess I didn't understand the dynamics of her marriage. Maybe the mechanic was what Arshell needed to get through this transition to menopause. I couldn't imagine what I was going to need.

Jordan was purchasing a house in Lower Merion,

which I had yet to see. I'd disappointed him several times when I'd had to reschedule appointments with the realtor. He'd already informed me that he wouldn't be around for the holidays because he was driving his grandmother down to South Carolina.

I'd been invited to numerous Christmas and Kwanzaa parties, and Trent had even invited me to a New Year's party Veronica was having at her loft in New York, but none of that interested me. Lyor had gone to Long Island to be with his family for Hanukkah. I was alone, and actually glad about it, because he'd become hard to resist.

Christmas at Daddy's with my grandchildren was the most fun I'd had in years. I'd spent the night so I could see their happy faces in the morning when they saw their presents and toys. Deirdre had long ago decided against the Santa Claus notion, and so we adults received all the credit. For Owen, I'd helped him buy the Denali truck he'd wanted. My gift to Deirdre was a vacation without the children—an all-expenses-paid trip for her and Owen to St. Thomas.

Daddy looked good and healthy. He'd stopped the chemotherapy, and Clara was always close by his side.

From Phoenix I'd received another coat, this time a knee-length shearling with mink cuffs, collar, and trim. When I'd asked him what was up with the coat for my birthday and now one for Christmas, he said that he didn't want me to have any excuses not to come to Chicago in the winter. Jordan and I had decided to exchange gifts when he returned, but for Lyor I had yet to come up with something that would in some way match what he'd given me for my birthday.

Since I had no date for New Year's, I gave Owen and

Deirdre a break and kept the grandchildren at my house for the night while they attended a party.

By the third of January I still hadn't heard from Jordan, and I began to worry that maybe something had happened to him. I tried him at home as I'd been doing for the last two days and was surprised when he answered on the first ring.

"Jordan, when did you get back? Why didn't you call me?"

"I'm sorry—I just got in this morning, and I've been wading through my mail and trying to unpack. How are you? Were your holidays good?"

"I'm fine. I missed you. Are you coming over?"

"Yes, a little later, though. I have to go out to the car dealer."

"You're getting a new car?"

"I thought I told you. Yes, I'm getting a BMW."

"I see. Well, that's nice. Will I see you and your new car later?"

"Sure. When are you going back to work?"

"Not until Monday."

"All right, I'll see you tonight."

Jordan never showed up that night, and it wasn't until a week later that I finally reached him at home.

"You've finally come up for air."

"What's that supposed to mean?"

"You told me last week that you were going to pick up a damn car, and I haven't heard from you since. I know you've gotten my messages."

"Yes, I have. Wait a minute, hold on."

I thought I heard him talking to someone in the background, but it was muffled. He came back to the phone. "Sasha, are you busy today?"

"Why?"

"'Cause we need to talk."

"You're talking to me now."

"I'd like to stop by your house this morning, if that's okay with you."

I couldn't wait to hear what his excuse was for being missing this past week, but the more I thought about it, the more obvious it became.

"Look, Jordan. If this is—"

"Sasha, I have to go, but I'll see you in about an hour."

Exactly one hour later, Jordan was ringing my doorbell. When I opened the door, he walked right past me and into the kitchen carrying a brown paper bag.

"I'm going to fix us some mimosas."

"What? Mimosas at ten-thirty in the morning?"

"It is a morning drink, isn't it?" he asked, while he mixed the orange juice and champagne.

"Fix it for yourself, I'm having coffee," I answered, returning to the living room.

With his champagne flute filled to the top, he sat in the chair opposite me. I was perched on the sofa, feet stuffed under the cushions.

"How were your holidays, Sasha?" he asked, nervously looking around the room.

"Jordan, please. Do you have something to talk to me about?"

"Look, I'm going to try to make this real simple." His voice was strained and his yellow face devoid of color. "I've been doing a lot of thinking over the holidays. Remember when I told you about Beverly and our breakup?"

"Yes, and?" I asked, remembering the woman I'd seen at church and met at the banker's event. Then the signs rushed back to me, the ones I'd ignored. How he'd stopped spending the night, the canceled dates and unanswered calls. I guess I'd been too wrapped up in my own life to care about what he was doing.

"The reason Beverly and I broke up was that she felt like I wasn't ready to settle down and at the time I wasn't. Then meeting you only proved to me that Beverly was right. I mean, you were exciting, you own your own business, and in the bedroom I've never had anyone who made me feel the way you do or who let me have my way with them. Sasha, there isn't a man alive who wouldn't want a woman like you."

"What are you saying?" I asked, looking down at my feet rather than at him.

"Well, now that I've had some time away from Beverly—"

"Time away? Jordan, where were you over the last few weeks?"

"Sasha, that's not important."

By now I was sitting on the edge of the couch. "You weren't in no damn South Carolina. You spent the holidays with Beverly, didn't you?"

"Sasha, this isn't easy, okay. Just hear what I have to say. You already knew I wanted to get married, and shit, you thought having my child was a joke when I asked you. I'm sure you know for yourself that you're not the marrying type."

Knowing full well what he'd been looking for, I asked anyway. "What the fuck is the marrying type?"

"Sasha, we've talked about this before. I want to get married, have children, and I know you don't want that."

"How do you know what I want? You never even asked me to marry you."

"There was no need to ask. You'd already told me you didn't want any more children, so why would I marry you?"

I didn't even try to hold back my tears.

"Listen, I enjoyed you, Sasha. We had a lot of fun together, and I do still want to work with Michael on publicity for the bank. But I have to settle down, build a family. Sasha, you're the one who's always talking about images, so I wanted to make sure mine was right for my next career move. And you, you just didn't fit in."

"What the fuck is that supposed to mean?"

"It means you're all about your business."

"About business? What the fuck were we doing then for the last year? All that fucking and spending time together wasn't business; at least, it wasn't for me. You know what, Jordan, just leave, okay? Just go and take your new wife, your babies, and your bank with you."

"You enjoyed every bit of it, and I do remember you getting paid very well for my business."

"Oh, I got it. I was some kind of good-time girl, but Beverly's worthy of marriage and having your damn babies." I didn't realize I was screaming until he said, "Sasha, quiet down, all right. You don't have to go off like that."

"Well, guess what, Jordan? After you and Beverly have your fucking babies and her ass is fat and boring, you'll be back in the streets looking for another Sasha Borianni, and I hope she takes you for all you got."

"Sasha, please. I wasn't trying to use you. It's just that she's what I'm used to. What *we* had is what we had, and I'll never forget you."

"Fuck you. Get the hell out of my house, you drunk."

Before he could say anything else, I jumped up from the couch and opened the front door to throw him out. That's when I saw his new 2004 BMW 745LI. I slammed the door behind him.

18

BUTTERFLIED

February 2004

I didn't realize until weeks later how much I'd come to depend on my relationship with Jordan. I'd been in a funk around the office, and when I finally told Tiffany that Jordan had dumped me, she simply said, "Sometimes being a bitch is all we have left."

I know it wasn't a wise thing to do, but one afternoon I called Trent on his cell phone.

"What's up with my favorite Philly girl?"

"Not much. You in town?"

"Sure am. Why, what's wrong?"

"You want to have dinner?"

"Damn right. I'll be at your office around six-thirty. I hope you'll be in a better mood by then."

When Trent arrived at my office, I was once again

impressed with his attire. He had on a black mock-neck sweater, black pants, and oxford shoes with a white suede cap toe. I was tempted to ask him where he was getting the money from to dress like that, but then I remembered where Veronica worked.

I hadn't forgotten how much Trent enjoyed a juicy medium-well steak, so I'd made reservations for us at Kansas City Prime. After a brief tour of the office, we walked hand in hand down Main Street to the restaurant.

"Tell me, gorgeous, what's going on in your life and why you are in such a funky mood."

"Not much, just work."

"Does that mean you would consider working for me?"

"Hell, no."

"Why not? You work for Phoenix."

"Trent, we are not going down that road again."

"I just thought I could get you in my life in some capacity. Are things still just business with Phoenix?"

"Yes."

"Something else must be going on, or you wouldn't have called."

"Me and Jordan broke up. Well, the truth is, he broke up with me."

"Why, Sasha? What did you do?"

"It's me. Look, Trent. If you're still holding some kind of grudge, maybe we should just forget this friendship thing."

"Damn, I just keep fucking up. I'm sorry again. Can we start over?"

I laughed at him. We were always starting over.

"How's this? What the hell is wrong with that man, giving up a woman like you?"

The waiter interrupted us to take our orders. Trent ordered the porterhouse steak, medium well and butterflied.

"What the hell is butterflied?"

"Aha, I surprised you with that one, didn't I. When you have a thick cut of steak, you have to make sure it's heated all the way through, right? So it's when they split the steak just enough to open it down the middle till you're able to see the pink inside. You get me, right, heated all the way through, pink inside, juicy?"

"That's enough, I get you very well."

We spent the next two hours talking about all the things going on in our lives. I didn't dare tell him about Lyor because he might've guessed that I'd started seeing him at the same time I'd been with Jordan. We had a good time, laughing and talking. At the end of the night we walked to my building rather than going straight to his car. While he used my personal bathroom, I checked for messages and pulled together some files to take home. Trent seemed to be taking a while, but when I turned to ask him if he was all right, I was surprised to find him standing directly on the other side of my desk.

"Sasha."

"Are you ready?" I asked, trying not to look at him, trying not to answer that look of lust his face held.

"Sasha?"

"Trent, you know we can't do this."

"Why not?" he asked, now kneeling beside my chair.

"Because it's not going to go anywhere. There are too many people in our lives, and our past is just too fucked-up."

"Sasha, be quiet and listen to me. I never stopped loving you even after everything that happened. I told you a long time ago that I forgave you. My stupid male pride is why I didn't come back for you sooner."

"But you said you'd never trust me again."

His hands held onto the sides of my chair. "Do you think I showed up at that awards banquet just to catch up? I knew you were there, and I knew you'd fight me, but Sasha—"

I didn't even wait for him to finish. I pulled him toward me until his lips touched mine. His arms wrapped around me, pulling me closer to him. I couldn't breathe, and I didn't want to. I closed my eyes and took in the scent of him, the feel of his beard against my face. My body was screaming for him. It had been so long.

"Sasha, damn, you feel good. I have to have you," he said, pulling me up from the chair and into his arms.

In the dark of my office we stood close, kissing, remembering, my hands playing in his beard. But I knew better; it would never work. I wasn't ready for Trent, and probably never would be. We couldn't go back; he'd never trust me.

I shook loose of him and stepped back, saying, "Trent, I can't. I can't right now. Please let me go."

"And if I don't?" he asked, pulling me back toward him, just holding me in his arms.

"You have to."

That night at home, after I'd unsuccessfully watched one of my tapes, the phone rang. I let it go into voice mail for fear that it might be Trent. But whomever it was hung up and called back again, twice. I snatched up the phone. "Hello."

"Ma, it's me. I'm taking Grandpa to the hospital. I found him in the bathroom throwing up blood."

"What? Where is he?"

"He's getting in the car now. Just meet me at Penn."

By the time I arrived, they had Daddy in an examination room and had already decided to admit him. He was groggy from the pain medicine they'd administered and could only whisper my name when I stood next to his bed, touching his cheeks. "Daddy, you're going to be okay, everything's gonna be fine."

He had a tube down his nose that Owen said was to remove any standing blood from his stomach. Owen went to get the attending physician, an Asian man who looked more like a student than a doctor.

"Ms. Borianni, I've spoken with his oncologist, and he'll be here first thing in the morning, but until then he'll be sleeping through the night, so I suggest you go home and get some rest."

"What, are you crazy? I'm not leaving until someone knows for sure what's wrong with my daddy!"

"Ma, Ma, calm down," Owen reassured me. "Listen, he's okay. Nothing's going to happen to him, they have him stabilized."

But we stayed for three hours, watching Daddy sleep until they took him from the emergency area and put him in a private room.

I drove back home, and after calling Arshell and crying about losing Daddy I took an antidepressant and crashed out on the couch.

In the morning I was awakened by a phone call from Daddy.

"Good morning, sweetness. I'm sorry about last night," he said, his voice weak.

"Daddy, you shouldn't be sorry. I'm getting dressed now. I'll be there in about half an hour," I told him, still in my clothes from last night.

"Don't rush 'cause they're getting ready to run some tests. Take your time."

I could hear someone in the background saying, "Mr. Borianni, you're not supposed to be on the phone."

I could barely place the phone on the charger, my hands were shaking so badly. I had to calm myself down. I picked up the bottle of Paxil, hoping another dose would get me through the day. While waiting for the pill to kick in, I called Kendra and told her about Daddy, then took a shower and drove to the hospital.

By noon Owen and I had met with the oncologist. The cancer had spread. I started crying, and Daddy, who already knew about it, was more worried about me calming down than the cancer.

"Ms. Borianni, you really shouldn't worry. It's not that bad. Luckily, it isn't in a lethal area. I'm going to prescribe a few chemo treatments, and after that we'll keep an eye on it."

I stayed at the hospital all day, even though Daddy repeatedly told me to go home. It surprised me when Lyor walked into the hospital room.

"How'd you know I was here?"

"I told you before that your receptionist has a soft spot for me."

Daddy was sleeping, so Lyor suggested we step into the hallway.

"Sasha, have you gotten any sleep?"

"I haven't been able to sleep."

"What good will that do your father? You want to stay at my house tonight, where it's quiet?"

"No, I'll go home later. Maybe I'll stay with Owen."

"Why don't you let me take you home?"

"I don't want to be by myself."

"I'll stay with you."

Back at my house Lyor helped me undress. I lay comfortably curled up in his arms while he watched CNN. I tried closing my eyes again, but I couldn't seem to get to sleep. He noticed my restlessness and said, "I'm going to run you a bath. That should help."

While Lyor was in the bathroom, I found the bottle of Paxil and took another one. I went into the bathroom when I heard him say the water was ready. And that was the last thing I remembered.

When I woke up, I was in my bed. The room was dark, and Lyor had covered me with my robe. He lay beside me in his boxers, lightly snoring. I was safe.

In the morning, while Lyor slept, I went downstairs to start a pot of coffee and wound up making a full breakfast of grits, sausage, and eggs. When I heard him upstairs in the bathroom, I called for him to bring my slippers down.

"That's a pretty big safe you have in your closet," he said, dropping my slippers onto the kitchen floor.

"I know. Phoenix put that thing in there for me years ago."

"I hope that's where you keep your necklace."

"All my jewelry is in there, along with some other stuff."

"How is your business with Phoenix going anyway? I haven't heard much lately."

"Things are at a standstill right now. The man who came forward now wants to withdraw his allegations, saying some shit about being confused."

"Job well done for you, I should say."

"I don't think it has anything to do with me."

"Believe me, Sasha, it has a lot to do with you. I've seen you on television with him, and it is clear to anyone who looks close enough that he follows your lead."

"Guess what?" I said, kissing him on the lips. "The last thing I want to talk about this morning is Phoenix Carter. Now, come and eat breakfast."

"Have you checked in on your father yet?"

"His doctor called a few minutes ago. Daddy will be in there for about two days. Then over the next two weeks they'll prepare his body for the chemo. The doctor is confident that Daddy will pull through just fine."

"Good. Now, after breakfast and before you go to the hospital, do you think we could go back upstairs, so I can help relieve some of that stress you're carrying around?"

19

SMOKE SCREEN

March

With Daddy out of the hospital, I traveled out to Los Angeles with Kendra to meet with Harry Bowen and his staff. Kendra and I had planned to do some shopping, and I was hoping to get some time to relax. I also had plans to meet Lyor in Vegas on Friday evening. By the time we arrived, it was eight o'clock West Coast time. Bowen had us picked up from the airport, and the driver told us that he was at our disposal during our stay in Los Angeles.

Once we had settled into our room at the Regent Beverly Wilshire, I got down to work while Kendra visited one of her friends from college. I made the usual round of checking voice mails, and since nothing was urgent, I decided to take a bath and order room service.

After bathing and slipping into one of the hotel's thick terry-cloth robes, I enjoyed a savory sautéed lobster-tail dinner followed by a delicious dessert of fresh berries and whipped cream. By the time I finished eating, I could hardly move, so work was out of the question. I called Daddy to make sure he was okay, but he wasn't at home. So I just lay there with my thoughts. Things were looking good for Phoenix. Brit Kostas was out of the picture, which meant the league didn't have any real evidence. All of which made Phoenix play harder, as Chicago was on a ten-game winning streak.

The next morning Kendra and I met with Harry Bowen. Our meeting took place in his private dining room at their office.

"Sasha, everyone on the production staff and our in-house PR person loves the work you've been doing. I think Philadelphia will be glad to see us come, at least until we get there next month and they see how we really shake up a town."

"It'll be fine. They won't care as long as you're spending money in the city. You will be able to attend the mayor's reception, I hope."

"Certainly, anything you've planned for me I'll be at. You know I don't usually spend too much time on these sets, but I've planned to stay in Philadelphia, and I was hoping I could get your personal assistance, at an additional fee, of course."

"Personal assistance?"

"No, not like that. I'm sorry. But hey, not a bad idea. For starters, I'll need a condo, maybe even a small house, somewhere in the city that's not high profile. I'll also need a car and a driver that can be on call at all times, one who is very discreet. And there could very well be some other things I'd need your help with."

"This shouldn't be a problem. Platinum Images is here to serve."

"No, it's not so much Platinum Images. It's you I want to handle this. Personally."

"How long will *you* personally need *my* services?"

"Three months. How does twenty thousand dollars sound? Does that help with your decision?"

"Decision made. When will you be ready for your first trip in?"

"That's what I like about you; you think like a man. I'll be there in three weeks. Do you think you'll be ready?"

"And payment?"

"Ten today, written to you personally, and ten when I arrive."

"I like doing business with you, Harry."

I was leaving his office when he added, "You know, Sasha, if this works out, you could make a lot of money out here in Beverly Hills."

"Harry, unfortunately I'm a Philly girl."

After two days in Beverly Hills with Kendra and a shopping trip that damn near blew my budget, I was on a short flight to Las Vegas.

Lyor was late picking me up from the airport, so I sat curbside listening to one of two garbled messages from Phoenix. Before I could return his call, Lyor pulled up.

It was obvious he'd spent plenty of time in the sun, judging by the dark tan he'd gotten. I couldn't wait to see the rest of his body. We were staying at the Mandalay Bay, and once we were in his hotel room he tried to muscle me into the bed.

"You act like you haven't seen me in months. We were just together a few days ago."

"Are you complaining about the way I take care of you?" he asked, pulling me close. He started biting at my stomach through my shirt.

"What's with you, and this?" I asked, touching his lips with my fingers.

"I'm the kitty, you're the milk. How's that to answer your question?"

"Okay, kitty, come and get me," I said, pulling my panties down from under my skirt.

"You don't even have to take them off, I'll eat right through them," he said, hoisting me onto the dresser. Before he could get to me, his cell phone rang. Pissed at the interruption, he answered.

"What do you want? I do not have time right now. I am in an important meeting."

While he listened, I continued to tease him, feeding myself to him, trying to make him take me while he was on the phone. But something wasn't right on the other end. He told the person to hold on.

"Sasha, not now. I need to take this call."

I was shocked at his abruptness. Just a moment ago nothing could've distracted him, and now he talked to me like I was some damn call girl. I went into the other room to unpack, but that didn't stop me from listening in on his telephone conversation.

"There is no more negotiating. Are you fuckin' crazy? Phoenix Carter made an agreement, and there will be no changes."

When he finished his call, I was no longer in the mood to be around him. I was more curious why he was discussing Phoenix's name, but his boorish mood warned me not to ask, at least not yet.

"Sasha, I am sorry about that. Forgive me. Now, can we go back to where we were, in the bedroom, on the dresser?"

"I don't think so. I'm hungry. Can we go to dinner?"

"Sure, I am sorry. It is all my fault."

"What was that all about anyway? International trading?"

"I would rather not discuss it with you. At least not right now."

I didn't like the look on his face. "Whatever you say," I answered.

We went downstairs to the famous Aureole restaurant in the lobby of the hotel. The atmosphere was like a circus with all its sprawling space and floor-to-ceiling wine tower, which made me think of Jordan. After making his wine selection, Lyor pointed out to me the "Wine Angels," women that flew on a kind of trapeze to retrieve your selection from the tower.

Our dinner was rather quiet. Lyor kept receiving phone calls that caused him to have to leave the table. I promised myself that if he took one more call, I wouldn't be sitting there when he returned. When he sat down, he grabbed both my hands firmly. "Sasha, I need to talk to you about something very important."

"What is it? Phoenix?"

"Yes, but not here. Let's go back upstairs to the room." He gestured for the waitress to bring the check. I tried to think of an excuse to get a moment to call Phoenix, but Lyor's behavior was becoming a little frightening.

Back in our suite, he poured us both a drink and shut off his cell phone.

"Sasha, do you trust me?"

"Not right now I don't." I thought of Tiffany repeatedly telling me that she didn't trust Lyor. "It's obvious you've been hiding something."

"Not anymore. Things have changed."

He stood up and went into the bedroom. When he returned, he sat down next to me, a small wooden box in his hand. He opened the box with a key. It was obvious that I'd gotten myself into some shit. Lyor was no longer just a man. He was an enemy who couldn't be trusted.

"Lyor, look. Just tell me whatever it is you have to say."

With the box unlocked, I looked inside. Laying against black cloth were about a hundred sparkling diamonds, no special lighting, just sparkling naturally. I was speechless as it dawned on me why Phoenix's name was possibly in this conversation.

I stood up. "Lyor, why are you showing me all this?"

"I think you know."

I didn't answer. I wasn't going to put Phoenix out there if it wasn't necessary.

"You don't have to say anything, but your client Phoenix Carter has something that belongs to me and my family."

"What the hell are you talking about? How can Phoenix possibly have something that belongs to you?"

"Sasha, please sit down."

I continued to stand because I didn't want to be caught off guard by whatever might be next.

"Listen, I brought you here because I needed to talk to you about something very important."

"I thought you brought me here so I could relax."

"Just hear me out. The issue is this. About five years ago

my brother Barry, who was a courier of expensive jewelry for celebrity clients, was killed while traveling from Chicago to New York. There were only a few people who knew that he'd be carrying some very special cut diamonds. You do remember, I told you my sister was a jeweler."

I didn't answer. I was too stunned by his story to respond.

"My brother's list of clients was very short, and as I think you already know, Phoenix Carter was among them."

"Lyor, you have to be crazy to think Phoenix had anything to do with your brother being killed."

He walked over to where I stood in the bedroom doorway. "You are the one person Phoenix listens to, and I need you to convince him to return my diamonds before he destroys what's left of his career."

"You bastard, you're the one that set him up. Don't tell me that's why I'm here, why we're here, why we've been together. That you planned this entire thing."

"No, I didn't plan anything. I have nothing to do with Phoenix's gambling worries or what's gotten into the news."

I didn't believe Lyor for a moment.

"Look, Lyor, I don't know anything about any diamonds, nor have I ever heard Phoenix talk about any. Anytime I've been with him he's bought jewelry from a store." I paused to see if he believed me. "But Lyor, I have another question."

"What's that?" he asked, closing the lid on the box, returning it to the room's safe.

"Has our relationship been about Phoenix all along?

"Sasha, how can you say that? Sasha, I love you."

"I'm sorry, but I just don't believe you."

"Well, then, you should believe this. Phoenix knows we're seeing each other, that we're here in Vegas together, and he's not happy."

"Right now I don't give a fuck about you or Phoenix." I turned my back and went into the bathroom, closing the door behind me. Leaning over the sink, I turned on the faucet and splashed cold water onto my face. I had to talk to Phoenix.

20

UNVEILING

Back in Philadelphia, I tried to reach Phoenix without success. I couldn't imagine why he wasn't returning my calls. Lyor had said Phoenix knew that we were in Vegas together, so why wasn't he calling me?

After a stress-filled day at the hospital with Daddy while he received chemotherapy treatments, all I could think about was going home and relaxing. I took a hot bath, turned on the television in my bedroom, and tried to watch sitcoms. It had been two days, and I still hadn't heard from Phoenix or Lyor.

I considered watching one of my tapes just for the hell of it. But before I could slide the box from under my bed, the doorbell rang. Nobody ever showed up at my house unexpectedly, so I immediately thought something might be wrong with Daddy. I looked out my bedroom window and saw a black town car. I headed downstairs, and when I reached the front door, I cautiously looked out the peephole. It was Phoenix.

"Where the hell have you been? I've been trying to reach you for two days," I said as I opened the door and let Phoenix inside.

"I came to pick up that package."

"That's it. You came to pick up the package. Haven't you listened to any of my messages? I know I didn't give you any details, but I'm sure you realized it was urgent."

I locked the door behind him.

"What's up?" he asked.

"You really don't know what's been happening, do you?"

"Sasha, what the fuck are you talking about?"

"I figured out LT is Lyor Turrell."

"Wait—what are you talking about? Don't tell me he's contacted you. I'll kill that motherfucker. Go upstairs and check that shit, make sure everything is still in there."

"Phoenix, I don't know how to tell you this, but I've been working with Lyor on the Panache casino project here in Philly."

"Man, I knew he was in Philly. You shouldn't have gotten yourself involved in all that. It's some very underhanded shit going on here."

"But Lyor's the one that you said was snitching on you to the NBA, the one asking for the diamonds—LT, remember."

"So what? It's over now. I'm giving them back to him. Well, I'm more or less bartering with him."

"Bartering with what?"

"With my career. You don't think all that shit stopped for nothing, do you?"

"I'm not sure if you're ready to hear what I have to tell you. Obviously somebody has been fucking with the both of us."

"What are you talking about?"

And so I told him, laid out everything about Lyor and me and about what happened in Vegas. When I finished, Phoenix didn't say a word. He picked up the cell phone and called out to the car to Trey. I opened the door for him.

"Sasha, get that stuff," he told me as he and Trey spoke in whispers in the kitchen.

I went upstairs, retrieved his envelopes, and brought them downstairs to him. He opened them up, counted all the diamonds, and dumped them all into one bag except for five, which he placed on my kitchen table.

"These are for you."

"I don't want them. I just want to know what you're thinking. I didn't know Lyor was—"

He cut me off and said to Trey, "Take these back to the hotel, I'll call you when I'm ready." Turning to me, he said, "What do you have to drink?"

I went to the cabinet and found the last bottle of wine from my days with Jordan.

"This okay?"

"It'll do. I gotta ask you. What were you thinking, fucking a white boy? I never thought you'd do some shit like that. Do you know who that motherfucker is? How he fuckin' tried to ruin me? You should've told me."

"Wait a minute, Phoenix, I didn't meet Lyor under those circumstances. It was completely innocent."

"Innocent my ass. You don't know him, Sasha. He knew good and well that if I knew he was fucking you, I would've never agreed to give that shit back. Things are going to have to change now."

I finished my drink and headed to the refrigerator for more. As I passed Phoenix, he handed me his empty glass.

"I don't want you involved in this any further," he said as he followed me.

After filling his glass, I offered it back to him, but instead of reaching for his drink, he reached for me. I couldn't move my lips to tell him no because he already had his hands under my robe.

"Sasha, I swear I didn't come here for this."

What was I to say? I'd been fucking the man that was trying to destroy him. I owed him that much, but even more than that, I wanted him. I wanted to finish what we'd started in Chicago.

He slid my robe off my shoulders and let it fall to the kitchen floor.

"You're not gonna fight me, are you?"

In answer to his question, I helped him undress. With his body exposed, I traced his tattoos with my tongue and moved him to see what new ones he'd placed on himself. I glided my fingers over his well-carved muscles and looked down to see if what I wanted awaited me.

"Take it, Sasha. It's yours."

He sat down on the couch and pulled me with him. Wrapping his hands around the locks of my hair, he used his knee to push my legs apart and brought my body down onto his, filling me up with his hard dick that slid so far up into me that I screamed out his name. We stared at each other as I rode him, hard, with him thrusting himself further up into me until I was screaming out his name, again and again, and unable to hold back, he buried his face in my breasts and let go.

Spent from the sudden burst of pleasure, I slowly climbed off him and lay my sore body on the floor.

After a few minutes he spoke up. "Sasha, we gotta talk about this Lyor shit."

"I know."

"You can't let him know you talked to me."

"What?" I asked, sitting up.

"Like I said, I need to play this thing out, and I need your help this one last time. You gotta continue to see LT until I figure out what I'm going to do. Can you do that for me, please?"

"Phoenix, I hate the sight of him. There's no way I can fake it."

"You have to. Please."

I didn't want to think about being with Lyor, not with Phoenix here so close to me. I wanted to pretend that Lyor didn't exist.

"If we work this out right, believe me, you could retire. Can you do that for me?"

"Are you leaving me tonight?"

"You want me to?"

I shook my head no.

The next morning Phoenix was gone before I woke up. I could smell what remained of him—the scent of his sex was coming out of my pores, and I knew that if I left the house everybody would smell him on me too, so I called the office and told Kendra that I would be late.

21

DADDY'S GIRL

May

Over the next week I tried to do as Phoenix asked and made myself available to Lyor, but luckily he was out of town for most of those days. When I did see him, I always found a reason not to sleep with him.

I was checking in with Harry Bowen on Friday afternoon when I received a hysterical call from Clara. An ambulance was at her house to take Daddy to the hospital.

"What happened, Clara?" I asked as I reached for my purse and keys.

"I don't know. He was doing okay, and then all of a sudden he starting throwing up. Oh, Sasha, I don't know what to do. I'm so scared."

"What are the EMTs doing? Can you put one of them on the phone?"

"No. They're strapping him to the stretcher. Sasha, can you hurry up, please?"

"Calm down, Clara. I'll meet you at the hospital." I ran out of my office, and as I passed Kendra in the reception area, I said, "Look, they just rushed Daddy to the hospital. Please call Owen right away. Tell him to meet me there."

Michael came out of his office and said, "I'll drive you."

Three days later and after way too many invasive tests, the doctors told us that Daddy's prognosis was not good. The cancer had spread to his lymph nodes. The only thing we could do was pray for him. Daddy had been made aware of all this and had willfully signed a do-not-resuscitate order. Owen and I tried to change his mind, but he insisted.

"Sweetness, if it's my time, then I don't wanna linger."

I had to respect his wishes.

Daddy made the best of his hospital stay. He had a swarm of visitors, all of whom acted as if he would be coming home. Clara never left his side, day or night. She sat there with him for every meal, feeding him food when he lost his appetite. It was a shame she'd come so late in his life. I truly believed that she was the only woman he had loved since my mother.

Daddy insisted that I not sit by his bedside waiting for him to die. But how could I not? To take off some of the pressure of driving from my home in Chestnut Hill to my Manayunk office to the hospital in University City every day, Lyor put me up in one of his apartments at the Left Bank. Regardless, the smell of antiseptic and soiled sheets stayed with me even in my bed at night.

Arshell and Wayne visited, and we tried to laugh and talk about Arshell getting through menopause. Arshell told me she'd finally broken it off with her mechanic. I was glad for her.

I saw Lyor every night when he was in town. On some of those nights I'd let him have me just to be close to someone. I had no idea what the situation was between him and Phoenix, but I was sure it would be settled as soon as Phoenix finished his run for the championship. Trent called me daily and had even come down to see me once or twice.

I'd lost my appetite and was surviving on vending-machine coffee and whatever Daddy's visitors brought. I knew I was losing weight by the way my jeans sagged in the ass, and I'd finally lost some of the roundness that surrounded my stomach. Right now nothing was more important than sitting at Daddy's bedside. I wanted to feel his touch and hear him call me "sweetness" for as long as I could.

I could tell my grandchildren felt death lingering. When they visited, they were scared to get too close to Daddy. But after a few visits they no longer cared about the tubes surrounding him, and without hesitation they climbed into bed with him. I knew then that it wouldn't be long.

During the second week of his stay he began to slip in and out of consciousness. He talked in incoherent sentences and even spoke of my mother, which brought tears as I hoped that somehow her spirit was in his hospital room with us.

It was on one of Daddy's better days that I felt the room get warm. I told myself it was just me until I saw Owen get up from the chair and move to sit on the side of Daddy's bed. I knew then that he had felt it, too. I convinced myself that the warmth was Daddy's love, covering us like a heavy winter coat.

"Daddy," I whispered, because I no longer had the energy to speak up.

In response, Daddy let out what sounded like a hum. He struggled to gather up the strength to give me a weak smile.

"Daddy," I said again, my eyes staring at his chest to make sure he was still breathing. His eyes fluttered open, and even though I couldn't see his lips moving, I could hear Daddy's voice. I sat completely still, holding my breath, my body rigid, to hear what he was saying.

"Sasha, I hear you. It's about time for your Daddy to go, sweetness."

"Daddy, you gotta hold on. You're the only daddy I got."

"Sasha, you gotta let Daddy go, you gonna be all right, I've seen to that."

Daddy's eyes were closed, and his lips hadn't moved, but I knew he was talking to me.

"You take care of yourself and find a good man to settle down with. You deserve it. You're a good girl."

Slumping down beside his bed, I screamed out, "Daaaaddddy, don't leave me. Please, please, Daddy don't go."

Owen reached out for me, but I shook him off. I was certain that if he touched me, I would shatter. I placed my hand on Daddy's chest. It was no longer moving. Owen placed his hand over mine. A nurse ran into the room, but I put my hand up for her to stay still and let Daddy go.

Owen called out to me, "Ma."

I turned to look at him. My son's face was streaked with tears.

"Is Grandpop gone?"

I turned back to Daddy to make sure his eyes hadn't

fluttered open one more time, but they were closed. I leaned over him, lay my face against his, wrapping my arms around his still body, kissing his eyelids, his cheeks, until I felt the warmth leave him. Daddy was gone.

For the week leading up to the funeral, other people took control of my life. I just followed where they led me. Arshell came to stay with me during those difficult days. Pastor Price offered to let us have the funeral at his church. Deirdre and Owen handled all the funeral arrangements.

For me the most important thing was to make sure Daddy was laid out in one of his finest suits. Clara and I picked out a gray sharkskin suit, a white French-cuffed shirt with his initials embroidered on it, and a black-and-gray silk tie. We finished the ensemble with gray crocodile shoes. He was beautiful.

When we arrived at the church in one of eight limousines, compliments of the limousine company Daddy retired from, I stood at the front of the line with Owen. The church pews were filled with a sea of mourners dressed in black, except for several women whose attire dotted the crowd with reds, purples, and oranges. I, too, had chosen a black suit topped off with a red Chanel scarf. Red had always been Daddy's favorite color on me.

I sat in the front row and watched as people walked past to view Daddy and offer their condolences to me. Family members both black and Italian, and Daddy's male friends, stood around the church as if guarding him.

When I turned to look around, I was surprised to see that some of my clients and media contacts were attending the service. Jordan was there, and even my ex-husband and his wife. And Phoenix had made time to come after he'd just received his fourth championship ring.

At the end of the service, when it was time to close Daddy's casket, I motioned to Clara to stand with Owen and me. Once again I felt Daddy's coat of love and protection drape across my shoulders. I looked at Daddy for the last time and told myself that there was no other like him, that the mold had truly been broken. I touched his cold hand, kissed his cold face, removed my scarf, and placed it beside him.

After the service everyone gathered at Daddy's house for the reception. Looking around at all of Daddy's friends, I wondered if I'd continue to see them. One by one, each of them handed me an envelope, and it went on like that until they'd all left the house. I felt as if I were a bride, the way Daddy's friends were giving me money. I was sure they knew I didn't need it, but it would be disrespectful of me not to accept it.

Phoenix also came back to the house after the funeral. I felt the tension between him and Lyor, but rather than feed into it, I let it go unacknowledged.

Trent was the most mature of the three men. He spent most of his time talking with Wayne and Owen. I caught him watching me throughout the afternoon, checking to make sure I was holding up. I was relieved that he hadn't brought along Veronica, who'd called during the week to offer her condolences. I felt a need to be close to Trent, so I asked him if he could take me home.

After my daddy's friends left, Phoenix told me he was leaving. I walked him to the door and asked him if he'd handled his business with Lyor.

"Don't worry about that. It'll be taken care of shortly."

I made my way to Trent and found him in conversation with Lyor.

"You two know each other?"

"You might say we're on opposing sides," Lyor said, wrapping his arm around my shoulders as if he were claiming me.

"How so?" I hated the fact that Lyor knew Trent, too.

"Lyor is like you, Sasha. He's all for the casino, and I'm against it."

"I see. Lyor, aren't you trying to catch a flight out to Richmond?"

"I've chartered a plane, so there's no rush. But I guess I should be going."

"Bye, Lyor. I'll see you on the battlegrounds," Trent said, shaking Lyor's hand.

An hour later Trent was driving me home in his Chevy Tahoe.

Trent pulled into my driveway, jumped out of the truck, and came around to my side to open the door.

"Thanks for bringing me home, Trent," I said as he helped me down from the Tahoe's high seat.

He led me to my door, and when I fumbled with my keys, he took them from my hands and opened the door.

Walking into my empty house, I decided I needed a change. I wanted to move. Trent took off his suit jacket and shoes, and while I looked through the mail and tried to listen to my voice-mail messages, he stopped me.

"Just sit down, okay."

I did as he said, kicking off my shoes and plopping down on the sofa.

"You know you're gonna be all right, don't you? But you can't just fill every minute with work."

"What else is there to do?"

"For starters, I'm here for you. I'm not going to let you keep hanging around that cutthroat Lyor Turrell."

"You know him that well?"

"Sure do. And I know a lot of shit on him. But don't you think about him right now. Hey, you still have that big bathtub?"

"Huh?"

Instead of answering my question, he went upstairs. I heard him running water in the tub, so I followed and found him naked in my bathtub.

"Trent, what the hell are you doing?"

"Bathing—what's wrong? Oh, you thought I was running this for you. Woman, my ass is dead tired."

"You're crazy, Trent," I said, getting out a washcloth and towel for him. I think I've made a decision about something."

"Making decisions when you're emotional isn't a good thing."

"That's when I make my best ones. I'm thinking about moving."

"Out of Chestnut Hill? You love this place."

"Yeah, I know. But I need some new surroundings. Need to let these old memories go. I've got to do something with my money. I can't leave it all to Owen. He'll buy a new car every year."

"And where would you move, Sasha? Further away from yourself?"

Trent climbed out of the tub and wrapped a towel around his waist. I followed him into my bedroom and asked, "What are you gonna put on?"

"Nothing," he said, tossing his towel onto the hamper, then stretching himself out across my bed.

"What are you doing?"

"Relaxing. You remember how, don't you?"

"Probably not," I answered, hanging my suit jacket in the closet. I put one arm over my shoulder to unzip my dress, but Trent had gotten up to do it for me. Seeing my sheer black stockings and garter belt, Trent exclaimed, "Damn, when you start wearing this sexy stuff!"

"Just something different. I got bored."

"Boredom does you well."

"Trent, listen. I don't want to . . . I mean, I want to, but I'm not ready."

"Get undressed and lie down. When and if we make love again, I want you to be willing."

I was willing, but I'd had too many men, and I wanted Trent to be different, special. I climbed into bed, and Trent pulled the covers over me. We lay there beside each other, Trent sleeping and me crying for Daddy.

22

CONFRONTATION

Two months after Daddy's funeral, I finally settled his estate. There had been two life insurance policies, a checking and savings account, and a metal box in his closet at home where he'd kept about $10,000 in cash along with stocks and bonds whose worth I had yet to find out. Daddy had named me as his executor, and he'd left a will with instructions on how he wanted his money to be distributed.

Thanks to Michael and Tiffany, Platinum Images was riding high. We'd hired another associate and an office manager. Bowen Entertainment was satisfied with our work, and the Funeral Directors and Morticians Conference had even come off without a hitch.

School was out, so Deirdre and Owen were making plans to take the children to Orlando for their first Disney World vacation. But the trip that Deirdre was really looking forward to was the Caribbean vacation I'd gotten them for Christmas. Everyone's life was moving along, but I had yet to find out how to step back into mine. I was considering selling the business, but if I did, I had no idea what I'd do with myself.

One day Lyor stopped by my office unannounced. Over the past month I'd only talked to him occasionally, so I had no idea if he and Phoenix had resolved their diamond problem. I really didn't care, as long as they were out of my house. When he walked into my office, I could tell that this wasn't going to be a pleasant conversation.

"I wasn't sure if you would see me."

"You could've called me."

"No, I couldn't have, because I've been leaving you messages," he said, closing my door behind him. "I haven't seen you since your father's funeral. Does that mean you've chosen Phoenix over me?"

"I didn't know I had a choice to make. Both of you fucked me."

"You might be right, because from what I hear, he spent the night at your house. But isn't that how you like it, Sasha?"

"I don't give a damn what you think you know. Your fight—if there is one—is with Phoenix, not me."

"Will you admit you knew about the diamonds all along?"

"Why don't you try admitting that you used me? Or are you going to say you came after me for the diamonds but wound up falling in love?"

"You don't understand. I could care less about those diamonds, they aren't worth shit. But I'd promised my family I'd get them back."

"And did you? Was it worth it?"

"Not if I've lost you, no."

"Lost me! I can't believe we're having this conversation. It was over between us when we were in Vegas. Get the hell out of my office."

"What do you want, Sasha? Money, another big account?"

"I'm sorry, Lyor, but there's never been a price tag hanging off my ass."

"Maybe you should tell that to Phoenix Carter. He's the one that's been paying for your services over the years."

"Get the fuck out of my office."

"Not without what I came for."

"And what exactly did you come here for?" I heard Phoenix say from the doorway.

Lyor spun to face the door. "Phoenix, what the hell are you doing here?"

"That would be my question to you. I thought we settled this."

"It is settled. I'm leaving."

"I don't think so, not yet," Phoenix said, blocking the doorway. Turning his gaze to me, he said, "Those were never Lyor's brother's diamonds that you had in your safe."

Lyor's eyes bored into me. "Sasha, don't listen to him."

"That wasn't even your brother. Was it, LT?"

"Sasha, you're a fool if you listen to him," Lyor said, trying to speak over Phoenix.

"He'd heard I had those diamonds and was trying to blackmail me with that bullshit about me shaving points. But his plan didn't work. His friend Brit Kostas was too greedy for money, and he didn't care where he got it from."

"Lyor?"

"Sasha, forget what this punk is saying."

"You know why he wants to forget? Because he wants you back, he can't stand the thought of losing all the way around. He'll get you whatever account you want, but I tried to tell him you weren't up for sale. But here he is, begging."

"Lyor, get out of my office. Get the fuck out of my office."

And from the doorway I heard Tiffany say, "Yeah, get the fuck outta her office."

And he was gone. I looked at Phoenix, not knowing what to say.

"When did you figure all this out? Why didn't you tell me what was happening?"

"I wasn't going to burden you with this shit. You had enough going on with your father."

"Thank you, Phoenix. I'm so sorry I doubted you."

"No, thank you for saving my career and holding on to those diamonds for me."

"Anything for you. You know that."

"What will you do now, from here? You have enough money—why don't you just move on?"

"I'm like you. I need the excitement. Plus, what can I move on to?" I asked, more to myself than Phoenix.

There was an answer to my question. I just didn't know it until I got in my truck that night.

EPILOGUE

SASHA

When I left my office that night, I'd given up on ever finding the love that had eluded me all my life. It just didn't exist. Maybe I needed a vacation, a year on an island helping poor people. Maybe I needed to be grateful. I certainly didn't need to work anymore. I had my $5 million stashed in the bank, and even more invested. It was no longer about the money. Now I finally understood what Phoenix had meant.

I sat in my truck and closed my eyes, imagining where I would go. Maybe I'd take a trip to Paris, Italy, places I'd never been. I'd surely seen enough of this side of the world. I started the truck, deciding that was exactly where I would go, tomorrow. I picked up the car phone to call my travel agent, but before I could dial, I heard the voice of a man say hello.

"Trent? How'd you get this number?"

"I have all your numbers. What are you doing this evening, Sasha?"

"You really wanna know?"

"I sure do, because whatever it is, I have a better offer."

"I doubt it. But since you seem so sure of yourself, here goes. I've decided to take a leave of absence and travel abroad for a few months. Now tell me you can top that."

"I'm adopting your plan. How soon do we leave?"

TRENT

Without knowing for sure that Sasha would take me back, I'd ended my relationship with Veronica. It hadn't been much of a relationship anyway. We'd been together when it was necessary for social events, but I knew I'd never really make her my woman. I couldn't. I'd never stopped loving Sasha, and I needed to know if it would work, this time, now that we'd both matured and had a chance to see what else was really out there.

I'd watched Sasha trying to resist me by telling me that it wouldn't work. Maybe a year ago it wouldn't have, but the men she had in her life weren't what she needed. They didn't love her. When I'd called her, somehow I knew she'd be ready.

SASHA

With nothing to lose, I left a message for Michael that I was taking an extended leave of absence and drove directly to Trent.

When I came through the door, it was easy to see we were both apprehensive about why I was there. But he made it easy, like he always did. He suggested I change into something comfortable while he pulled together something to eat.

Without asking any questions, I did as he told me. When I came back downstairs in one of his T-shirts, he was in the kitchen, so I sat on the couch and waited.

"Hey, you in there? The food's ready."

I went to the kitchen where he was heaping broccoli on his plate, next to a T-bone steak.

"This is nice. Veronica must really appreciate you."

"There is no Veronica anymore."

When he said that, I hoped he'd invited me there for the same reason I'd come. But I had to know for sure.

"Trent?"

"What is it? You don't eat steak anymore?"

"Trent?"

"Sasha, you know why you're here, or else you wouldn't have come."

TRENT

No woman except Sasha had ever made me nervous. When she walked in my door, looking tired and exhausted, I could see why she wanted to leave the country, leave whatever had brought her to this point. But what she didn't know yet was that she didn't need Paris or Italy or any of those places. I had what she needed.

I couldn't rush her, though. After she showered, I waited until she came to the kitchen. She wore one of my white T-shirts that covered just enough of her. I wanted to take her in my arms right then, but I had to wait until I was sure she wanted the same thing.

"Sasha," was all I could get out as I slipped my hands under the T-shirt and felt her skin. "Is this what you want?"

"I want it as long as it's forever."

SASHA

Finally he came to me. Trent knew that he could've had me a long time ago if sex was all he wanted. But I wanted more, so for the first time I'd waited, waited for him. And the wait was worth it.